Savage Mountain

Books by John Smelcer

Fiction

Edge of Nowhere
Lone Wolves
The Trap
The Great Death
Alaskan: Stories from the Great Land

Native Studies

The Raven and the Totem
A Cycle of Myths
In the Shadows of Mountains
The Day That Cries Forever
Durable Breath
Native American Classics
We are the Land, We are the Sea

Poetry

The Indian Prophet
Songs from an Outcast
Riversong
Without Reservation
Beautiful Words
Tracks
Raven Speaks
Changing Seasons

SAVAGE MOUNTAIN

JOHN SMELCER

Leapfrog Press
Fredonia, New York

Published in 2015 in the United States by
Leapfrog Press LLC
PO Box 505
Fredonia, NY 14063
www.leapfrogpress.com

Printed in the United States of America

Distributed in the United States by
Consortium Book Sales and Distribution
St. Paul, Minnesota 55114
www.cbsd.com

First Edition

ISBN: 978-1-935248-65-1

Library of Congress Cataloging-in-Publication Data

Smelcer, John E., 1963-
Savage mountain / John Smelcer. -- First edition.
pages cm
"Inspired by true events."
Summary: In the summer of 1980, brothers Sebastian and James Savage decide to climb one of Alaska's highest mountains to prove themselves to their father but, instead, through testing their limits, learn that now matter how different they may be, the strongest bond of all is brotherhood. Includes discussion questions.
ISBN 978-1-935248-65-1 (paperback)
[1. Mountaineering--Fiction. 2. Brothers--Fiction. 3. Adventure and adventurers--Fiction. 4. Fathers and sons--Fiction. 5. Alaska--History--20th century--Fiction.] I. Title.
PZ7.S6397Sav 2015
[Fic]--dc23
2014044521

for James, still on the mountain

Acknowledgements

The author would like to thank Bard Young, Rod Clark, David Roberts, Amber Johnson, Dan Johnson, Steve McDuff, Matty McVarish, and Lisa Graziano.

"It's not the mountain we come to conquer, but ourselves."
—Sir Edmund Hillary
(the first person to summit Mount Everest)

Savage Mountain

For almost a million years the mountain had been thrusting itself skyward in violent upheavals, buckling and folding the crust from the collision and one plate riding over and consuming the other, upending the very earth itself. At more than 16,000 feet, its summit is eternally shrouded in snow and ice, tangled in clouds, and blasted by raging storms. In the brief summertime, its alpine glaciers melt, creating the headwaters of streams and rivers forever eroding the valleys and floodplains. So insurmountable, the unconquerable mountain destroys anything that dares to rise up against it.

Some fathers are like a mountain.

Saturday, May 29, 1980

THE BASEBALL BAT JUST MISSED smashing Sebastian's brains out of his head. Instead, the tip of the bat punched a hole through his bedroom door.

"Holy crap! You could have killed me!" he shouted when he saw the hole, which was big enough to put his fist through.

"Stop ducking and I'll finish the job," replied James, choking up on the grip and pulling back to swing again.

Sebastian acted quickly, throwing all his weight against his brother, the two crashing against a hallway wall and wrestling for control of the bat. He managed to pull the weapon free of his murderous brother's grasp.

"Stop now!" he said, trying to defuse the situation. "Seriously! Chill out!"

But James wouldn't listen. He sucker-punched Sebastian in the stomach, knocking the wind out of him, and ran into the kitchen. While catching his breath, Sebastian heard drawers opening and closing. James appeared a moment later with a long butcher knife in his hand.

For the next several minutes, fourteen-year-old James tried to slash or stab his brother, who was almost two years older. Sebastian managed to keep furniture between them—the coffee table, the recliner, the dining room table and chairs—while James lunged at him with the knife.

"Cut it out, man! Someone's gonna get hurt," Sebastian warned while avoiding the wielded blade.

The brothers had been fighting each other for most of their life. But matters had gotten worse, escalating to the point where one or both could be seriously harmed, even killed. Although Sebastian was older than James, they were almost the same height and weight.

During a failed lunge, Sebastian managed to grab his brother's arm and twist his wrist until he dropped the knife on the floor. Sebastian kicked it away. After that, the fight spilled down the stairs and out onto the front lawn. At one point James picked up an old weathered two-by-four from a stack of discarded lumber beside the garage. He swung it like a baseball bat, trying to strike his brother in the ribs. But Sebastian turned and hunched over, just in time, so the eight-foot board broke in half over his back. The snapping sounded like breaking bone.

Sebastian jumped his brother and knocked him to the ground. The two were rolling on the grass slugging each other when a police car pulled up and a policeman stepped out.

"Alright, break it up!" he commanded, with one hand patting his black, holstered night-stick.

The brothers struggled to their unsteady feet. James gave Sebastian a shove and Sebastian pushed back so hard that James tripped and fell.

"That's enough!" shouted the policeman. "What's going on here?"

"Nothing," replied the brothers, both with bleeding lips or noses and torn and grass-stained shirts.

"It looks to me like you two were trying to kill each other."

"We're brothers, sir. That's all. Just brothers," replied a nervous Sebastian.

"Yeah, I figured as much. How old are you two?"

Brothers

"I'm sixteen," replied Sebastian. "But I turn seventeen this summer. He's fourteen."

"Yeah, but I'll be fifteen in a couple weeks," said a visibly angry James. "Jerkwad here didn't mention that."

The cop shook his head in disbelief.

"You guys are too old to be acting like children. Where do you live?"

James pointed to the green two-story house behind them.

"This is your house?" the cop asked.

Both boys nodded, wiping away blood with the backs of their hands.

"I have two brothers myself and we used to fight like hell all the time. Are your folks home?"

"No, sir," replied James. "They went shopping."

"Well, you can't be out here disturbing the whole damned neighborhood," replied the cop, noticing the woman across the street looking out her living room window. "Take it inside."

"Yes sir," replied both boys, relieved.

The brothers never did resume their fight. Truth is they didn't even remember why it started in the first place. Instead, they cleaned up the mess they made before their parents came home, righting things they had overturned, like a lamp, the coffee table, and a magazine rack full of *Popular Mechanics* and *National Geographic*. Sebastian patched the hole in his bedroom door and painted it with a partial can of off-white paint he found in the garage. When his father later asked why he had painted the door, Sebastian replied that he just wanted to make his room look nicer.

His dad bought it.

Sunday, May 30, 1980

"PICK IT UP, YOU DAMN SISSIES!" the insistent father shouted at Sebastian and James, who were struggling to lift a fifty-five-gallon drum full of gasoline into the bed of a pickup truck.

"But Dad, this weighs over three hundred and sixty pounds," complained Sebastian, having already done the calculations.

"We've already tried a hundred times," James exaggerated, wiping his dirty hands on his jeans and then examining a broken fingernail.

"Shut up and get it in there, you crybabies!" the father scowled. "Pull up your little girl panties and act like men. How'd I end up with losers like you two?"

The boys struggled again, managing to get the lip of the drum onto the edge of the high tailgate, but then it slipped when they tried to lift the bottom. The problem wasn't so much the weight itself as the awkward shape and the sloshing contents of the drum. It would have been manageable had the drum been equipped with handles.

"Get under it!" the father said sternly. "Use your legs, you friggin' wussies!"

But each time the boys almost got it up, James would lose his grip and the drum would fall, and the boys would jump back for

23

fear of the sharp rim smashing their toes. Sebastian was strong for his size. He trained with weights and ran five miles three days a week, even in winter when it was 30 or 40 degrees below zero—the air burning his lungs, ice forming on his wispy, teenage moustache. On some days he ran as far as ten or fifteen miles. Although as tall as his older brother, James was nowhere near as strong.

The father watched the boys make several more futile attempts.

"Move out of the way, damn it," he grumbled and shoved James aside.

From behind his crouched father, James bit his lip and gestured as if he would punch his old man in the back of the head. With a furtive glance, Sebastian shook his head, and James lowered his balled fist and turned away, stomping his foot in anger.

"I don't know why I thought you two girls could do anything. "Here," he said squatting beside the drum, "let a *real* man show you how to do it."

"Why you always gotta treat us like crap?" asked Sebastian.

His father looked up.

"Because life is hard. You need to be tough. Things don't always turn out the way you want them to. Now get down here and help me, Priscilla."

Sebastian helped tip the drum against the lip of the tailgate, and then he crouched like his father.

"On the count of three lift and slide it in at the same time," said the father, their faces close from their hunched position over the barrel. "Use your legs."

On the third count the two were able to hoist the back of the drum waist high.

"Push! Push!" shouted the father. "Use your muscles!"

Sebastian dug his feet into the ground and used his shoulder to push. The drum slid into the truck bed and rolled heavily against a side wall, sloshing from side to side until finally settling.

The father slapped his hands together, wiping away dirt and rust.

"See! How hard was that? Now, you two pansies load the other one by yourselves and come in for dinner when you're done. And make sure the bung is on tight."

"But, Dad, it could take us an hour to load it by ourselves," said Sebastian, already hungry and exhausted from trying to load the first drum.

"I don't care if it takes you all night. You two cupcakes don't set foot in the house until it's loaded in the truck. You hear me? I'll make men of you two wimps yet."

But Sebastian and James knew that it really didn't matter if they managed to load the drum or not. Whenever they failed at something, their father was quick to demean them. When they succeeded, he dismissed their achievement just as quickly. The bar was always nudged higher, like a summit they could never reach. The brothers were trapped in a world in which they could never triumph.

After his father left, Sebastian used a long screwdriver to make sure the bung was on tight enough so the gas wouldn't spill when the drum was on its side.

After failing several times to muscle the drum into the truck, Sebastian got an idea. He remembered the stack of used lumber beside the garage. James sat on the tailgate while Sebastian picked through the pile, returning moments later with three of the strongest eight-foot-long two-by-fours. He leaned each one against the tailgate, spacing them a little over a foot apart.

"Give me a hand," he said to his younger brother.

Together, they tipped the drum onto its side and with some difficulty managed to roll it up the planks and onto the tailgate. It was an easy matter after that to manhandle the drum into position and slide it into the bed alongside the other drum.

"That's how you get it done!" exclaimed Sebastian cheerfully as he closed the tailgate.

Sebastian was always like that: using his brain over his muscles. His father hated that.

He worried Sebastian would grow up to be a poet or something.

After returning the boards to the pile beside the shed and slapping each other a high five, the brothers proudly walked into the house in time for dinner. When they sat down at the table their father stared at them hard, then he stood up from his chair and walked over to the front window where he could see the truck with both barrels in the bed. He sat back down and ate his meal without saying a word.

As he always did after dinner, their father sat in his over-stuffed, brown-fabric recliner in the living room reading the newspaper. The wall behind him was covered with plaques, photographs, certificates, and framed newspaper stories about him from the old days. He called it his "I Like Me Wall." The most prominent item was a picture of him standing beside a four-star general next to a jeep with its tires caked in mud. The fireplace mantle and an adjacent bookshelf were lined with old high school football trophies.

Sebastian walked in to get his school books.

"Tonight's garbage night, Dumbass. Take the trash cans out to the curb," demanded his father without even looking up from the newspaper.

"But I have to work on an essay for school," said Sebastian, talking to the wall of newspaper. "Can't James do it?"

"It'll only take a few minutes. It's your job this month. Just do it! And stop blinking all the time. What the hell is wrong with you?"

He was used to giving orders. He had served in Vietnam during the early years of the war. He had even won medals for valor. Sebastian knew when it came to his father's commands there was no room for discussion or compromise, only *Do as I say or suffer the consequences.*

But Sebastian didn't do it right away. He decided to push the envelope and delay a bit. Instead, he worked on his essay for almost an hour and then called a classmate to talk about the assignment and compare notes. Afterward, he went downstairs into the garage to exercise for half an hour. He tried to train a little every day, at home or in the school weight room, where mostly wrestlers and football players trained. He had a rack of iron weights, a couple sets of dumbbells, and a sturdy bench-press bench in a corner. Although Sebastian was slight, around five-foot-six and weighing only 130 pounds, he could bench-press 225 pounds, 240 on a good day. He could deadlift every weight he had in the garage, an unbelievable 400 pounds—more than three times his own body weight. Although he had only been competing for about two years, he held numerous records in the sport.

When Sebastian finally came up for bedtime, exhausted from a good workout, he noticed mountainous lumps beneath his blanket. He thought maybe it was his brother hiding there to surprise him, but the shape didn't look like a person. He pulled back the blanket to find that two large bags full of garbage had been emptied onto his mattress, ripe and disgusting, with coffee grounds, egg shells, spaghetti scraped from dinner plates, pork chop bones, bacon grease, moldy bread, wilted lettuce, and greasy black banana peels. It took him over an hour to pick up all the trash, take it out to the curb, and wash his funky-smelling sheets and pillowcases.

Monday, June 1, 1980

"HEY, CAN I HAVE A RIDE TO SCHOOL?" James asked Sebastian, who was sitting astride his idling motorcycle cinching his helmet chinstrap.

Sebastian loved his green and white Suzuki 385GT street bike. He had been bagging groceries since he was in seventh grade, mostly a couple days a week after school and on Saturdays. He made tips only, but on a good Saturday he sometimes made as much as a hundred dollars in cash, mostly in ones and quarters. When he turned sixteen, he bought a used Datsun pickup truck with a dinky four-cylinder engine only a little bigger than a motorcycle engine. The little engine didn't have much power, but it got over thirty-five miles per gallon. The truck was painted metallic gray, and it sported cool chrome moon hubcaps. It also had a black snap-on bed cover. He and his best friend, Andy, had installed a cassette player and more powerful speakers than the tinny ones it came with. He had a brown faux-leather box full of his favorite cassettes, which included ABBA, Elvis, Neil Diamond, Tony Orlando and Dawn, The Bee Gees, Quarterflash, Super Tramp, Johnny Cash, and Jim Croce. Sebastian's taste in music was retro before it was cool to be retro.

He'd bought the five-year-old motorcycle only two weeks

before, just as the weather warmed up enough for biking, which, in the interior of Alaska, was pretty late in the season.

"Sure, grab the other helmet," he said with a smile.

While James was in the garage looking for the helmet, Sebastian took off for school, laughing aloud as he leaned into the turn from their street onto the main road. He sometimes gave his brother a ride in the truck, but he wasn't about to have his brother sitting behind him with his crotch pressed against his back and his arms wrapped around his waist. That place was reserved for girls. Besides, James could still catch the school bus, which would be by in about five minutes.

"Take your hat off," said Mr. Betters, the Western civilization teacher, pointing at the Harley Davidson cap on James' head. "We don't wear hats in school."

In fact, almost everything James was wearing was Harley Davidson paraphernalia. He wore a heavy black leather jacket that creaked when he moved, and he had one of those long, black leather wallets connected to a belt loop on his jeans by a chain, both articles adorned with Harley logos. More than anything, James wanted to be a biker and join Hell's Angels. But, unlike his older brother, he didn't have enough money to buy a motorcycle, and besides, he couldn't legally drive one until he turned sixteen, which was more than a year away.

James begrudgingly removed the cap.

Mr. Betters stood up from his desk with a stack of papers in his hands.

"I have your tests from last week. I'm glad to say that some of you did very well," he said, glancing at Sebastian sitting in the front row wearing a gray sweatshirt with the words "Latham High School" in purple and gold. "And some of you did *not*," he said, emphasizing the last word.

James knew the stuffy teacher was talking about him. Although he was a freshman and his older brother was a junior, they were in the same elective class. It was the only time they had ever been in the same class in their entire lives. Sebastian was the teacher's pet, always earning A's and always knowing the right answer to questions.

"Excellent work, Mr. Savage!" Mr. Betters exclaimed as he handed Sebastian his test with a large 'A' written in red ink. "And I like your school pride," he said pointing at the sweatshirt.

The teacher was less enthusiastic when he returned James's test.

"Do you listen to *anything* we talk about in class?" he said, as he handed James his paper with a "D-" written at the top. "Couldn't you at least *try* to answer all the questions? Why do I even bother?"

After returning all the tests, Mr. Betters stood with his arms across his chest before the chalkboard.

"Now, as you all know, this is the last week of school. That was your last test, but you all still owe me the five-paragraph essay I assigned about the last chapter we read. Please get out your papers and pass them to the left. And make sure your name is on them."

Everyone in class handed in a paper . . . everyone, that is, except for James, who never looked up from his Pee-Chee folder with the words "Western Civ. Sucks" scribbled across the ubiquitous sketch of a sprinting athlete surrounded by other doodling and the names of hard-rock bands like AC/DC, Led Zeppelin, Black Sabbath, Van Halen, Cheap Trick, and Kiss. On the back cover he had written in large outlined letters: "Highway to Hell."

While the other students robotically handed their stapled essays to the person to their left—his brother included—James quietly added two exclamation marks to the class name on the front of his folder.

Later, as everyone scrambled out of the classroom after the bell to head to third period, Sebastian stopped his brother in the hall.

"Hey, Bro, what'd you get on the test?"

James reluctantly pulled out the crumpled paper from his jacket pocket and showed it to his brother.

"Bummer, Dude," Sebastian said, patting his brother on the back in a kind of mock sympathy. "Sucks to be you."

James didn't ask what Sebastian got. He already knew. Everyone knew Sebastian was a straight-A student on the Honor Roll. All James could muster before they went their separate ways for the rest of the day was a defeated, "School sucks!"

James had barely walked up the stairs when he got home before his father jumped on his case, speaking as though he had rehearsed what he was going to say beforehand.

"Your teacher called. He said you didn't turn in your final assignment, a term paper or something. He said he didn't think you would pass without it."

James stood there, steeling himself, expecting to turn into a punching bag any minute.

His mother came out from preparing dinner in the kitchen.

"What's going on?" she asked.

"Nancy here didn't turn in the last assignment for one of his classes."

A south paw, James clenched his left fist.

"My name isn't Nancy," he said very quietly.

"Stop mumbling and speak up like a man," demanded his father in his drill sergeant tone. "What's the matter? You got mush in your mouth?"

"I said I'm not a girl," James replied, enunciating each word clearly and deliberately.

"Stop calling the boys girls," said the mother, who didn't often chastise her husband.

But she turned and walked back into the kitchen after her husband gave her a scowl as fearful as a slap in the face.

"Your teacher said he'd accept a late paper from you. Now go to your room and don't come out until you've written it. And I want to read it when you're done."

"But dinner's in half an hour," James complained.

"I don't care. Get to work."

James stood at attention, snapped his heels together, and saluted his father.

"Heil Hitler!"

Instantly, his father smacked him upside the head so hard that the boy's ear rang and he grimaced in pain.

"You better show me some respect, you little prick!" exclaimed the father, stabbing his index finger against the boy's thin chest. "I'm sick of you! I'm sick of your attitude. You can't do anything right!"

His father's words slashed through James' leather jacket like switchblade.

"You're a goddamn weakling! You'll never be half the man I am!"

The boy's face turned beet-red, his knuckles white as a snowstorm. Finally, the abuse was too much to bear.

"I'm not a girl!" James erupted, taking a swing at his father and landing a glancing blow on the shoulder. "I'm not weak!"

The father fought back.

For several minutes, father and son—ages thirty-eight and fourteen-going-on-fifteen—grappled on the green shag-carpeted floor, punching each other and pulling each other's hair while James' mother screamed for them to stop.

Tuesday, June 2, 1980

"FIGHT! FIGHT!" SOMEONE YELLED, while another student ran to find a teacher.

By the time a teacher arrived, James was fighting with three seniors from the varsity football team, each one of them outweighing him by forty or fifty pounds. All four had bloody noses and blood on their shirts. There were red smears on the gray hallway floor where sneakers had slipped on the blood. Maybe fifty students stood around watching the melee, cheering it on.

"Come on, man! Get him! Hit him! Kick him in the balls! Punch his lights out!"

No one coming on the scene would have had any clear notion for whom exactly the outbursts were meant.

The teacher, who taught English in a classroom two doors down, didn't know who to grab.

"Break it up! Break it up!" he repeated, at first without much success.

But whenever the teacher grabbed one of the football players by the arm to pull him away from the fray, James took advantage of the moment and punched the player in the head. Finally, Mr. King, the assistant principal, arrived to help, and, together, they managed to stop the fight.

"It's all over now. Go to your scheduled classes," Mr. King instructed the assembled mob. "You heard me. Get going."

Then he turned to address the three jocks.

"You guys okay? Anyone need to see the nurse?"

All three said they were okay.

"Alright, go wash your faces and then get to class," said Mr. King. "But you, Mr. Savage," he said using a beckoning index finger, "come with me."

Neither said a word as they walked down the long hallway lined with lockers broken intermittently by windowed doors leading into classrooms. As they passed the main doors, James looked down at the tiled floor, which listed every year the school had been in existence, beginning with 1956, the year they had closed the old Fairbanks High School and opened Latham. When he stepped over the 1960 tile, James thought of his father, who had graduated from Latham in that year. When he stepped over the last year, 1979, James imagined that his year would be listed on the floor in a few years.

That is, *if* he graduated.

During the quiet walk, James pondered what was going to happen to him. This was the fourth time in the semester that he had been caught fighting, each time requiring a little talk with Mr. King. When they arrived at the principal's office, James plopped down in the chair across from the desk.

"You should name this chair after me, or something," he said, chuckling at his own joke.

Mr. King wasn't amused.

"What is it with you? Do have a death wish? Are you high?" Mr. King asked while closing his office door. "I just don't understand why you keep getting into *fights*," he said, emphasizing the last word as he sat heavily in his cushioned chair behind his dark desk. "Your brother never gets in trouble."

James stared at the floor. He could feel the brass knuckles inside his leather jacket pressing against his ribs. He wondered if the assistant principal could see the bulge from across the desk. Sometimes he carried a switchblade knife instead of the brass knuckles.

"I'm not my brother," he whispered, clenching his fists, trying to hold back the anger he could feel welling up inside him.

"How's that?"

"I'm not my brother!" James shouted, and brought his fist down on top of the desk so hard that a small framed photograph of a woman holding a little girl fell over.

"You certainly aren't your brother," replied Mr. King, righting the toppled photograph. "I just sent a news release to the newspaper with a list of the students who will have earned a 4.0 GPA this semester. Your brother's name is on it."

"*La-dee-dah*. You gonna marry him, too?"

"Always the tough guy. Always the bad-ass with the whole leather-jacket-biker routine. It's like you always got something to prove, or you're just plain suicidal."

Still looking down, James noticed blood on the white part of his black-and-white sneakers. He wondered whose it was. He was worried that the assistant principal might ask to check his jacket for drugs and find the weapon and the sandwich baggie with a couple joints' worth of weed.

"For Chrissake," Mr. King continued, leaning forward to make his point, "you're going to get in a lot of trouble if you keep up this crap after you turn eighteen. I mean *legal* trouble, like jail time, a criminal record."

Without looking up, James touched his bottom lip. It felt swollen. He could taste blood inside his mouth, irony and salty.

"Do you hear a word I'm saying? I'm trying to understand you. I'm trying to help you."

For the first time, James looked up, not at the man sitting behind the desk in front of him, but at the framed diplomas and degrees hanging neatly on the wall behind him.

"You went to the University of Alaska?"

Mr. King turned around to look at the diplomas.

"Yes. That's right. I earned my bachelor's and my master's there."

"Sebastian wants to go there when he graduates. Our dad went there, too. He also went here."

"I know all about your father. Everyone in town does. You have every reason to be proud."

James cringed.

"A lot of the records he set playing quarterback here go way back in the late fifties. He set all kinds of records. Some still stand today."

"Yeah," replied James, shrugging. "You don't need to remind me. I see the trophies and the pictures of him with his greased-back hair in that glass case by the main entrance every day."

"You know, your father led his teams to the state championship three years in a row?" Mr. King boasted as if it were his own father he was talking about. "Three in a row! That's something."

"Yeah, yeah," replied James, unmoved. "He has all these pictures and trophies and plaques in the living room and in his den, including a bunch of medals and crap he got when he was in Vietnam.

"I have a lot of respect for your father. He's a war hero, son . . . an amazing man. A real patriot. *A man's man.* You should be proud."

"I guess," is all the reply James could muster, his conflicted feelings about his father churning away in his stomach till he felt like throwing up all over Mr. King's nice desk.

"You would do well to be more like your father."

James glared into the assistant principal's eyes. He wanted to jump across the wood desk, rip the man's arm off, and beat him with it.

Oblivious to the boy's intention, Mr. King continued.

"What about you, James?" His tone was sympathetic, as though he felt he was making some headway, establishing a connection with the troubled teen the way he was taught in his night classes in education. "What do you want to do with your life?"

"I don't know. All I know for sure is that I'm tired of everyone comparing me to my brother. I'm not like him. I'm also sick and tired of people telling me what a great guy my dad is. They don't know him the way I do. If they only knew the things he does to . . ."

James stopped mid-sentence.

Mr. King studied the troubled boy across from him and tried to think of a response.

"What do I want out of life? I'll tell you," James continued, his voice slow and far away. "I just want to be left alone."

"What do you mean by that? Are you having problems at school?" Mr. King asked, leaning closer, genuinely concerned.

"My problems with school don't mean crap, excuse my French."

"Then what is it? Are you having problems at home?"

"There's no problem. I play my part."

"What part is that?"

James was quiet at first, looking down at the linoleum floor again, counting the large gray and black squares, thinking about his father and how to endure him, about things he knew and would never share with anyone. Tears welled up in his eyes before he spoke.

"My father and I have our roles. He tries to break himself against me, and I do the breaking. Pretty simple. I can deal with it."

A look of concern descended on the middle-aged man's face.

"Do you want to talk about it?" he asked.

"No."

"What about your brother? Does Sebastian have trouble with your father?"

"Yeah, sure. Of course. We both do. We just deal with him differently."

"What do you mean?"

"Nothing," said James, standing up from the chair. "Forget I said anything. Can I go now?"

"We're not finished," replied Mr. King, motioning for James to sit back down.

James complied reluctantly, slumping lazily in the wooden chair.

"Sit up straight. Listen to me, James. I can't have you starting fights in my school. This is the fourth time this semester. I have to suspend you, even though there's only three days left until summer vacation. I'll have to call your folks."

James's shoulders drooped, and he shook his head in defeat.

"Great! Just what I need. My dad's gonna *love* that," he said sarcastically, emphasizing the world *love*—a word, for him at least, that never belonged in the same sentence as the word *father*.

James walked the two miles home, kicking empty cans along the way, and thinking about what his father was going to do to him after Mr. King told him about the suspension. He still had bruises from their fight only the day before. Halfway home, walking by a bank, he saw a small bird fluttering on the sidewalk in front of one of the large windows. He could see a little tuft of gray feathers stuck to the glass about seven feet up, and he reasoned that the bird must have flown into it, the way birds often fly headlong into windows. The bird was on its side with its eyes closed, its beak cracked at the tip, its clawed toes opening and closing slowly, as if they were trying to grip a tree branch.

James knelt to look at it closer.

"I think you knocked yourself out, Little Fella'," he said softly.

He watched it for a minute. He could tell that it was breathing, and the eye facing up tried to open a few times.

"I can't leave you here while you come to," he said in a sing-song fashion. "Something might eat you."

James gently scooped up the small bird and carried it in the warm cup of his hands, occasionally stroking its tiny head with a fingertip and speaking to it, comforting it. By the time he was almost home, it was clear the bird had died. With his bare hands

James dug a shallow grave in the dirt at the edge of a parking lot and buried the little bird, placing a handful of dandelions atop the mound.

When he arrived outside his house, James could hear his father shouting from inside the living room. He crept beneath an open window so he could hear.

"I was supposed to be something!" his father yelled, and then James heard a loud crash, like something being thrown against a wall.

"I wasn't supposed to sell insurance all my goddamn life!" he screamed.

James heard another crash.

A moment later, James heard his father's heavy footsteps going down the stairs to the front door. He dashed around the side of the house and hid, peering around the corner. He saw his father slam the front door, stumble on the cement steps to the driveway, and climb into his truck, slamming the squeaky door. His father started the engine and slammed his fist against the dashboard before backing out of the driveway hurriedly, then screeched the tires on the pavement as the truck vanished around a turn in the street.

James went upstairs and saw the mess his father had made. All of his father's trophies were on the floor. Pieces of wood and silver-and-gold-gilded plastic were everywhere. Little figurines of poised quarterbacks lay faceup and facedown, some still with the football in hand, some without. Empty beer cans were strewn amid the shattered trophies.

For the next half hour James cleaned up the mess, placing all the broken pieces in a box.

BROTHERS
PILLAR OF THE COMMUNITY
APPLES & ORANGES
NOWHERE MAN
THE PLAN
DAY ONE
DAY TWO
DAY THREE
DAY FOUR
DAY FIVE
DAY SIX
DAY SEVEN
DAY EIGHT
THE RECKONING

Friday, June 5, 1980

THE LAST DAY OF SCHOOL AT Latham High School was like the last day at any high school: students cleaned out their lockers, returned their textbooks after removing the well-marked, ubiquitous brown-paper grocery bag covers, signed year books, exchanged phone numbers, hugged, shook hands, and said goodbyes for the summer. Boyfriends and girlfriends made promises to stay together no matter what. Not one student looked back at the school building after dashing out the wide-open doors into the springtime day.

That evening, Sebastian's mother showed him the article in the local newspaper listing the students who had earned a 4.0 GPA. The list was small for a school of over a thousand students. She had circled Sebastian's name.

With an expression of pride, Sebastian showed the article to his father, sitting as usual in his recliner watching the nightly news. His father glanced at the paper for an instant before handing it back to his son.

"So what? You wanna medal?"

A look of disappointment replaced the previous hopeful expression.

"No, I just thought you'd, you'd . . ." Sebastian tried to get the words out.

"What? Speak up. Quit mumbling. You got mush in your mouth?"

"I thought you'd be proud of me."

His father grabbed the newspaper from Sebastian's hand and flung it across the room, the pages separating in midair, fluttering all over the room like a fistful of dry leaves.

"What's there to be proud of? Huh? Because you got good grades at school? You're *supposed* to get good grades at school. Do you think anyone puts my name in the newspaper every time I do something good at work?"

"I just . . . I just, just tha, tha, thought . . ." Sebastian stuttered the way he sometimes did when he was nervous or agitated around his father.

"Stop stuttering! You sound like a damn imbecile."

Sebastian should have known better. Only a couple months earlier, he had broken a world record in weightlifting for his age and weight. There had even been a story in the newspaper with his picture and everything. But when Sebastian showed it to his father, the man crumpled it up and tossed it into the fireplace. Sebastian watched as the paper burst into flames, vanishing as quickly as his sense of accomplishment. More than anything, a boy wants his father to be proud of him. In their myriad and desperate attempts to win their father's approval, many sons try to be *like* their father. Some eventually *become* their father, for better or for worse. Some break the cycle of abuse and crushing indifference; some become yet another link in the long chain forged by years of abuse—an unending legacy passed down from father to son, like a grandfather's pocketknife or pocket watch.

Sebastian promised himself that if he ever had children, he would tell them how much he loved them every single day of their life. He would never do the terrible things to his children that his father had done to him. He would build them up, not tear them down.

Try as he might—an overachiever extraordinaire—Sebastian

was coming to realize that nothing he could ever do would be good enough for his father.

"You think you're better than me?" his father had said as the paper burned. "Listen to me, punk. You'll never amount to anything! I'm ten times the man you'll ever be."

That night, Sebastian's mother came into his room before bedtime with the newspaper. She had cut out the small article listing those students with straights As.

"Here," she said, sitting on the edge of the bed and handing him the small piece of paper. "Keep this in your yearbook. It's part of the story of your life. I'm sorry your father is so . . . *harsh*," she said, after thinking of the right word.

Sebastian took the clipping, looked at it, and then looked at his mother.

"Why don't you help us?" he asked. "I mean, why don't you *do* something?"

His mother looked him in the eyes.

"What am I supposed to do?" she said sharply. "I can't divorce him. I don't have a good job. I couldn't support us. Where would we live? We wouldn't have a nice house like this."

Her brown eyes began to tear up. Sebastian could feel his mother's sadness that she was unable to stand up for her sons.

"But isn't our happiness more important?" he asked.

"I don't have a choice," she said, wiping her face and standing up to leave. "You boys just don't appreciate how hard your father works to provide for us. You need to learn to deal with him on your own."

"Do you love him?"

His mother paused in the doorway, only for a moment, before she walked away without answering.

Around noon the next day, Saturday, the Savage family drove to a nearby park to attend the annual employees' family picnic hosted by the insurance company where Mr. Savage worked. Even though it was cloudy, James wore dark sunglasses. Their father introduced the boys to Mr. McCready, one of his colleagues who had just moved to town from Seattle a week earlier.

"That's some firm handshake you got there," he said to Sebastian. "Your father has been so helpful since we moved here. You're really lucky to have such a good father."

Sebastian and James looked at each other, rolling their eyes.

Mr. and Mrs. McCready had two teenage daughters about the same age as Sebastian and James. They were beautiful, with long red hair and freckles. Both girls were tall and slender. During the picnic, the four teenagers sat at their own table, apart from the adults, the brothers sitting across from the sisters talking about school and the classes and teachers the girls might have in the fall. The whole time the brothers flirted with the sisters, asking if they could bring them another soda or a hotdog or a slice of watermelon. They wiped the picnic table seats with their shirt sleeves before the girls sat down.

"Your dad sounds really nice," said the older one, whose red hair was longer than her sister's.

Sebastian and James exchanged glances again.

"Yeah . . . well . . . don't believe everything you hear," said James.

"What do you mean?" she asked.

"Nothing," replied Sebastian.

James wanted to change the subject.

"So, what kind of movies do you like to see?" he asked the younger sister, sitting across from him. "*The Empire Strikes Back* is playing at the theatre. Did you see *Star Wars*?"

Both girls nodded that they had.

When it was time to leave, Mr. Savage came to get the boys. He seemed in no mood to linger.

"Let's go," he commanded.

"But, Dad, can't we stay a little longer?" Sebastian pleaded, subtly nodding his head at the girls.

The girls smiled up at the man.

The Plan

"Yeah, just a few more minutes? Please?" added James, holding his hands together as if he was humbly praying or begging for mercy.

The youngest girl giggled at the gesture.

"I said *now!*" the father snarled, seizing both boys by the ear and yanking them gruffly off their seats. He looked around to see if any of the adults were watching.

"You think those girls want anything to do with pathetic losers like you!" he said just loud enough that the girls heard.

After closing the car doors, Mr. Savage turned around and smacked Sebastian with the back of his hand.

"Next time I tell you to do something you better shut up and do it! You hear me?"

Sebastian glared back at his father without answering, biting his lip so hard it bled.

On the drive home, fuming in the back seat and rubbing his cheek, Sebastian whispered into his brother's ear.

"That's the last straw. We gotta do something. I can't take any more of this."

Back home after the picnic, Sebastian was preparing to wash his motorcycle on the front lawn, where the policeman had stopped the fight with his brother only a week earlier. He had already rolled out the garden hose and turned on the faucet. He had even brought out a radio, an old towel, a rag, and a bucket full of warm, soapy water with an orange sponge floating on top of the white suds. He had just turned on the radio when his brother came out.

"Can I help?" James asked.

"I'm not paying you anything," replied his defensive older brother.

"I figured as much. I'm bored."

The early summer afternoon was cloudless and windless. Summers in the interior of Alaska are much warmer than folks from the lower 48 imagine. The record is a sweltering 99 degrees, set in the decade after the Klondike Gold Rush. Both boys wore shorts and tee shirts. It felt good to be outside on such a nice day listening to the radio, which was playing Cheap Trick's "I Want You to Want Me," which was topping the charts.

"What are you gonna do this summer?" asked James, while washing the spokes of the rear tire.

"Don't know," replied Sebastian, scrubbing the front tire rim. "Work a couple days a week at the grocery store, read a few books, exercise, jog, chase girls. What about you?"

"I got a big nothing. I'll probably just sleep in 'til noon every day. Maybe mow some lawns and wash some cars for spending money. Mostly, I'll be trying my best to avoid Dad." James touched a spot beneath his right eye with two fingertips.

Sebastian looked at his brother's face, at the black eye from the blow their father had given him on learning about his suspension from school.

The boys were quiet for a few minutes, each focusing on washing the motorcycle, thinking.

Sebastian broke the silence.

"I have an idea about that," he said.

James stopped cleaning.

"About what?"

"I have an idea of how we can avoid Dad and make him regret he ever called us a pair of wussies."

"Yeah? What is it?"

"I was thinking we could climb Mount Sanford."

James dropped the sponge and stood up to stretch his legs. Sanford was one of the tallest mountains in Alaska, and therefore one of the tallest in North America. The brothers had talked about climbing it one day, but James had always thought Sebastian meant when they were older, like in their twenties.

"You think Mom and Dad will let us do that?" he asked.

"Of course not. But what if they didn't know?" replied Sebastian, drying off the gas tank.

54

The Plan

"How's that?"

"We tell them we're going to some summer camp, like that wilderness survival camp we went to last year. We tell them we'll even pay for it ourselves."

"You think they'll go for it?"

"Think about it, Dufus," Sebastian said. "What parents wouldn't want a week or two away from their kids? They could go on vacation or walk around the house naked if they want. We tell them we're going to camp or something like that, and instead we go climb the mountain. I already got a camp brochure to show them. We already have all the gear. We just need to buy food for the trip. I'll take photographs to prove to Dad what we really did. He can raise hell all he wants, but the proof will be there. It's something he's never done, and I think if we pull it off, he'll back off. He'll have to respect us."

James could see that Sebastian had clearly thought through his plan.

"I like it. It's devious," he said with a sly smile. "And stop calling me a dufus!"

Truth be told, the plan wasn't as rash as it sounded. While their friends were like most teenagers—fearful of getting lost in the woods, always watching television or playing video games, on the phone all day, or hanging out at the mall—Sebastian and James felt at home in the wilderness. Much of their lives, especially the summers, had been spent in the woods. Both boys knew how to climb and rappel, how to survive in the wilds of Alaska.

For years, their father got rid of the boys by sending them to summer camps where they learned mountaineering. They had even gone to an arctic survival camp during the first week of January, when the temperature plummeted to 50 degrees below zero. The wind chill factor drove the temperature down to an unbearable -70 or even -80. From their years of training, the boys had learned how to traverse steep chasms from one side to the other and how to master a rappelling tower. Sebastian had even mustered the courage to learn the Australian Crawl, a technique in which the climber runs face-forward down the cliff wall instead of the more traditional method of facing upward during the slow, backward descent. Only two summers earlier, Sebastian had spent ten days at a climbing and outdoor survival school in the Sierra Nevada Mountains of Northern California. He had become an ardent climber, buying his own equipment, mostly used and outdated.

At one camp, both boys had learned how to navigate on glaciers, ice climb, and how to avoid dangerous crevasses and moulins. Both had studied basic first-aid training. More than once, despite their mother's vociferous concerns, their father had let them go backpacking or hunting on their own for days. Sebastian had shot his first caribou the previous fall when he and James went up into the Crazy Mountains about sixty miles north of Fairbanks toward the Yukon River. Over the years, Sebastian and James had had harrowing encounters with bears and wolves, encounters they would never share with their parents. But most importantly, the only time the brothers ever really got along was when they were out hunting, fishing, or climbing together.

Alaska's wilderness was the glue that bound the brothers together.

"Mom would have a cow if she found out!" James laughed.

"Then we make sure she *doesn't* find out . . . neither of them. When it's time, we'll load all our gear into the back of my truck under the bed cover so they can't see it."

"There's only one problem with your plan," said James, looking thoughtful. "Won't we need bottled oxygen to climb that high?"

"No, Dillweed. It's only a little over 16,000 feet. High altitude sickness doesn't really affect climbers until around 18,000 feet. You don't need those bottles until you get into the Death Zone.

"What's the Death Zone?"

The Plan

"Above 8,000 meters there's not enough oxygen. The air is so thin that it affects your ability to think clearly, and you feel tired all the time. Your blood becomes so thick that it's hard to keep warm. A lot of climbers have died in the zone from cerebral edema or pulmonary edema."

"What's pulmonary enema?"

"Cerebral *edema* is caused by swelling of the brain, which causes a loss of mental and motor function, kind of like being really drunk and disoriented."

James grimaced.

"And pulmonary edema affects the lungs so you can't breathe. It's much more common."

"I hate the stupid metric system. How many feet is 8,000 meters?" asked James.

"Around 25,000 feet," replied Sebastian, doing a quick calculation in his head. "You'd need bottled oxygen on K2 or Everest, but even then, some people have made it to the top without it."

James seemed impressed.

"How tall are K2 and Everest?" he asked, knowing his brother would have the right answer, the way he always did in Mr. Betters' Western Civilization class.

"About 28,000 and 29,000 feet, respectively, give or take," replied Sebastian.

"How do you know all that crap?"

"Because I read books, Dickwad," said Sebastian. "You should try it some time."

James stuck his tongue out in defiance.

"You're so funny . . . looking," he replied.

For a few minutes, while Sebastian finished drying the rest of the motorcycle with the towel, the brothers talked about their father and how he was always putting them down for one thing or another.

"What's his problem anyhow?" asked James. "Why's he so mean all the time? Why does he hate us so much?"

"I don't know," replied Sebastian, looking at the cloudless sky. "I wonder about that every day of my life."

"Me, too."

"I wish I had an answer," said Sebastian, still looking to the blue horizon. "But I think he hates us because he hates everything. He's angry at the world for one reason or another. Maybe his father never loved him. Maybe he's just broken, and he can't love anyone, not even himself. Maybe it's because we're not like him. We don't even look like him. We look more like Mom, especially you with your little breasts," Sebastian laughed.

James punched his brother in the shoulder.

"I don't have breasts!"

"Seriously, though. I'm always trying to make him proud of me, always thinking if I do *this* or *that* maybe things will be different. Remember how I ran for class president last year? Why do you think I do all the things I do?"

"I just figured you were a nerd."

"Ha, ha," Sebastian replied sarcastically. "But nothing I ever do is good enough for him. Nothing ever seems to make a difference. I don't know why I waste my time."

"I know what you mean," said James. "You're like a little kid on a playground always yelling to your mommy to see what amazing thing you're doing, 'Look! Look! Look!' You're always trying to win his approval. I gave up trying a long time ago. I could care less. I can't wait to move out."

But Sebastian knew better. James acted like he didn't care, but he knew that deep down inside his brother wanted their father's love and approval just as much as he did. The one thing Sebastian could never figure out—and perhaps he never would—was *why* his father didn't love them, *why* he hated them so much. The way he figured it, if anyone in the whole world *had* to love a person, it *had* to be his or her parents.

It just had to be.

When the boys were done washing and drying the gleaming

motorcycle, James turned off the faucet and rolled up the garden hose while Sebastian put away the plastic bucket and hung the towel, rag, and sponge out to dry.

"So, when do we leave?" asked James, in a tone resembling enthusiasm.

"The brochure says the ten-day camp begins on the first day of July. That gives us three weeks to get ready."

DAY ONE

Tuesday, July 1, 1980

THE DAY OF THE BROTHERS' JOURNEY arrived sooner than expected, the way thin ice suddenly stretches out across lakes in late fall, signaling the imminent arrival of winter. Bright and early on the first day of July, Sebastian and James waved goodbye to their mother as they climbed into Sebastian's small, gray truck. Their father could care less. He was glad to be rid of the boys for ten days.

"Got everything?" asked Sebastian, as he fumbled to insert his key into the ignition switch.

"Yep. Let's blow this joint," replied James, like a biker setting out on a freewheeling, coast-to-coast road trip.

As he drove down the quiet street, Sebastian watched his home become a small and harmless object in the rearview mirror. When he turned onto the main road, the tiny house vanished altogether, as if it no longer existed at all.

For the first time in a long time he felt free.

Sometime in mid-afternoon, after driving more than 200 miles of heaving paved highway—dodging moose, porcupine, and occasional caribou along the way—the little gray truck stopped at the abrupt end of the bumpy, gravel road that stretched from the highway nearly twenty miles to this remote spot. Before them, and down a steep bank, was a muddy, braided river, fed by melting glaciers. Instead of one main channel like most rivers, these wide, shallow, glacial-born waterways sometimes have dozens of shifting channels twisted across a wide floodplain, giving the impression of hair braids. The muddy color comes from the silt the river carries in its veins. The river was a couple hundred yards wide.

Several miles to the east was the mountain they had come to conquer.

From where they sat, staring in awe out the cracked windshield, Sebastian and James could see two of the three massive prominences that made up the Wrangell Mountains, which seemed to thrust themselves abruptly and unexpectedly from the relatively flat landscape around them. As mountains went they were quite young—not even a million years old—pushed skyward by volcanic activity. Sanford, the mountain they had come to climb, towered above them at 16,237 feet. To the south, eighteen miles away, Mount Drum rose to 12,010 feet, almost a mile shorter in stature. Behind Sanford, and unseen from the brothers' vantage point, was 14,163-foot-tall Mount Wrangell. Of the three, only Wrangell was historically volcanically active. A thin, wispy plume of smoke perpetually belched from its snowy summit. Among the Indians living in the region—The People of the Copper River—it was said that the plume was the campfire smoke of the dead, whose spirits dwelt on the mountain.

Sebastian studied Sanford's South Face, rising over 8,000 feet in a mile, a thousand feet higher than Everest's Kangshung Face. Few mountaineers had attempted the South Face. Instead, he planned to ascend the North Ramp, the most common route to the summit.

The brothers said nothing as they took in the spectacle of the snow-covered peak thrust into the cobalt sky, a few benign clouds floating on the horizon. Privately, both were imagining themselves at certain points along their planned route or standing on the summit, looking down at the green world below, exhausted from the climb yet bursting with a sense of joy and triumph.

Day One

Neither imagined the dangers that awaited them.

Sebastian grabbed his Polaroid camera and took a picture of the mountain. The brothers watched as the image materialized before their eyes. When it was fully developed, Sebastian placed the photograph on the dashboard and gestured to his brother that it was time to go.

For the next half hour the boys pulled their gear from the back of the truck, taking a quick inventory of their equipment while swatting away mosquitoes. Some of their gear was homemade, like the snow shovels. Sebastian had bought two square-nosed garden shovels at a garage sale and simply sawed off most of the wooden handles' length. He sanded the cut ends until they were rounded and drilled a hole through which he tied a lanyard so he wouldn't lose them. He spray-painted the handles bright orange so they could be easily located in snow.

Most of the climbing equipment was old school. Each carried two coils of climbing rope, one fifty meters long and one sixty meters long. Dozens of carabineers—a mixture of open gate and locking—and a variety of twenty-year-old used metal pitons hung from carabineers on a bandolier made of a short piece of rope, which was worn over a shoulder and across the chest the way a Mexican bandito wears his bandolier full of cartridges. The two piton hammers were regular hammers, the claw almost straight, not the tightly curled claw for easy nail pulling—each with a lanyard tied through a hole in the hickory handle, which Sebastian had also painted orange.

Instead of modern harnesses, the boys had learned how to tie a "Swiss seat" using a piece of rope about eight feet long to which the climbing rope was hooked through a heavy-duty, locking carabineer. Sometimes they used two carabineers, just to be on the safe side. The extra resistance also helped to control the belay, when one a climber safeguards another by controlling the slack end of the rope during ascents or descents.

It's an important responsibility; a matter of life or death.

The belayer must watch the climber's every move, offering slack when needed, taking it up so as not to leave too much in the event of a sudden fall. If a belayer takes his hands off the rope even for a moment, to swat a mosquito or scratch a nose, for example, the climber could fall to his death. The further a climber free-falls the more the sudden stress on the rope, the carabineers, and the steadfast pitons—not to mention the human body—when the fall is finally arrested. It's a simple law of physics that every climber knows by heart: force equals mass times acceleration. Many climbers have been hurt, even killed, by the sudden snap of the rope during a fall. To combat that, modern ropes stretch somewhat under the weight of a freefall, thereby reducing such impact. Climbing ropes in the old days were dangerous because they didn't stretch. Maintaining the correct rope tension is at the heart of rope work when climbing. When two mountaineers are too far apart to communicate by words, the belayer and the climber exist in a kind of symbiotic relationship. Part of the art of climbing lies in the belayer's ability to maintain harmony between the climber's actions and intentions and his or her own keen observations.

Mountaineers entrust their lives to partners and teammates a hundred times a day. Some of the strongest and most enduring friendships are forged from having shared the perils of mountain climbing. Some of the greatest regrets are of friends left on the mountain.

Sebastian and James each had a pair of white Army surplus "bunny boots," ungainly and heavy, but warm to 60 degrees below zero. Their sleeping bags were green Army surplus "mummy bags," also good to extreme low temperatures. They each had a thin, blue, rolled-up sleeping pad to keep their bodies off the snow, and their tent was nothing more than a cheap, orange pup tent, to which they could tie extra guy-lines during high winds. Even their green backpacks were Army surplus. Their climbing helmets were brightly painted construction helmets bought secondhand. Aside from their climbing ropes, they each carried a couple hundred feet of white parachute chord for hoisting or lowering their packs and gear. Their pockets stowed two pairs of tinted downhill ski goggles to protect their eyes from blasting winds and snow blindness. Sebastian stuffed a blue winter coat into his pack. When he wore it, he looked like a blue Michelin Man. James packed a red one.

All in all, their expedition was funded on a shoestring budget, no modern gear like walkie-talkies, spring-loaded cams, or Jumar Ascenders. They carried no official expedition patch or any kind of flag to plant at the summit.

Their only relatively expensive equipment consisted of two used ice axes and the two pair of used crampons, removable traction devices with sharp metal points or teeth strapped to the soles of boots to aid mobility while walking or climbing on packed snow or ice. Both pairs were specialized for mountaineering, with ten or twelve angled points, including two front-pointing teeth to aid in vertical climbing. The climber can jab his toes into the ice face to gain a temporary foothold. Before purchasing the used equipment at a gear swap, Sebastian carefully examined every inch for signs of excessive wear or damage. He wasn't taking any chances with his or his brother's life by using crappy gear. He never bought used ropes. You never know what they've been through or how well they've been cared for or how many times they've been over-stressed in falls or washed and dried improperly.

For food, both backpacks included packets of dehydrated foods, instant pancake mix, packages of Ramen noodles, rice, powdered soup, powdered milk, and powdered eggs; and oatmeal, granola, dried fruit, and caribou and moose jerky they had made themselves. They also included chocolate bars for quick energy, instant coffee, and bouillon cubes for making hot broth. Aside from the food, there was a small cooking pot and a collapsible cooking stove powered by small cans of Sterno. Most climbers used compact gas stoves, but those were expensive. Sterno was low-tech but lightweight, reliable, and heated just as well. Besides, a person could burn twigs inside the stove just as easily. The supplies also included waterproof matches and long-burning emergency candles. And, of course, each brother carried a plastic flask for drinking water—made by melting snow—stored inside his parka to prevent the water from turning back to ice. Sebastian had a basic first-aid kit in his pack, including a suture needle and thread should the need arise. Almost as important as any piece of equipment, each pack included two rolls of toilet paper in sealed plastic bags, the rolls squished flat to save room. It was important to keep the packs as light as possible without sacrificing what was needed to succeed . . . and survive.

Both boys wore a whistle attached by a string to the zipper on their lightweight jackets to ward off any grizzly bear ambush while hiking through brush at low altitudes and to help find each other should they become separated in a whiteout or an avalanche. And each carried one item of luxury. Sebastian brought a collapsible Polaroid camera so he could take pictures to prove to their father what they hoped to accomplish. James brought a harmonica.

After snugly lacing their leather hiking boots with sole patterns that looked like waffles, the boys tied their white bunny boots to the outsides of their packs alongside their helmets in such a way that they wouldn't swing and bounce every time they took a step. They wouldn't need them until they were high up in the snowfields. Sebastian locked the truck doors and hid the keys under the frame, using a short piece of wire to secure them to the rear brake line. He made sure his brother saw where he hid them, just in case.

"Well, let's get to it," he said, hoisting his heavy pack onto his shoulders and adjusting the bulky weight. "We should be able to make it to the base and set up camp by bedtime."

There was no need to use words like *night* or *nightfall* because in mid-summer, such as it was, the sun never really sets on Alaska. That's why it's called Land of the Midnight Sun. The boys would be able to see well enough to climb no matter the time of day. Only exhaustion would dictate when it was time to sleep. Only their rumbling stomachs would tell them when it was time to eat.

With some difficulty, James put on his pack and cinched tight the waist belt.

For a long minute the brothers stood side by side looking at the mountain—three miles high—with a single billowy cloud snarled on its craggy peak. Sanford was 3,000 feet taller than the Eiger and 1,500 feet taller than the Matterhorn, both in the Swiss Alps. From where they stood, they could see the daunting South Face with its 8,000-foot vertical rock ascent, one of the steepest in the world. Their planned route would avoid the unnecessary dangers of such a technical climb.

After slinging the coiled ropes over head and shoulder, the boys clambered down the steep bank and made their way across the river, forging across the shallowest riffled channels where the swift icy water came up no higher than their knees. By the time they made it to the far bank, neither could feel his toes. They took a break to empty water from their boots, wring out their soggy socks and pants, and warm their feet in the summer sun.

"How long do you think it will take us to reach the top?" asked James, rubbing his feet.

Sebastian glanced at the mountain before replying.

"I figure we can make it to the summit in maybe four or five days from here. Take us less time to get back, coming downhill and all. Maybe just three. That gives us a couple extra days just in case some bad weather sets in."

"That doesn't seem likely," replied James, looking at the sunny sky. "It must be almost 80 degrees today. It doesn't snow in July."

"That's true. But mountains make their own weather. You never know what's up there." Sebastian looked up at the mountain again.

"It can be calm as can be down here, but the winds up there could be howling mad. I imagine it's below freezing up there right this minute."

James shuddered at the thought.

Sebastian marveled at the extraordinary contrast of the landscape—the brown, flowing river, the pinkish flowers of fireweed and red rose hips growing along the gravel banks and sandbars, the scraggily green forest and the far green hillsides with their patches of alder, and above it all, the bright snow-covered mountain rising into a cloudless blue sky—all melting into a kind of symbolic landscape not of this world, like something out of a fantasy book with impossible vistas. Sebastian wasn't intimidated when he looked at the frozen slopes and ridges of the mountain. Instead, his mouth was dry with excitement, and he felt his heart ache in the presence of the inexpressible beauty of it all.

"It's so beautiful," he said, eager to begin the rites of piton and hammer.

James stopped rubbing his feet and studied the faraway peak. He swallowed hard and his heart felt as though it were held in a vice.

"What am I getting myself into?" he muttered, so low that his brother didn't hear what he said.

"What'd you say?"

"Nothing."

After the sense of feeling returned to their feet, the brothers set off again. They hiked along the riverbank for almost a mile before turning right, toward the east, and following a small stream in a narrow dell that became increasingly steep and boulder-strewn. At some point, they scrambled out of the little gulley and made their way up to a ridge, where gray lichen grew on the rocks, and where pikas and marmots scurried out from their dens among the stones. The few brush-like trees, tortured and stunted, crouched against the wind.

Day One

Walking behind James, Sebastian couldn't help but notice his brother's underwear protruding above the beltline of his blue jeans. As all mischievous boys are wont to do, Sebastian grabbed hold of the white elastic band with both hands and yanked. James turned around and chased Sebastian, trying to reciprocate. After he'd pulled his underwear out from between his butt cheeks, they resumed their trek; this time Sebastian was in front, keeping an eye on his brother.

"Hey," he said, turning around, "at least I didn't give you an atomic wedgy."

"What's that?"

"It's where I pull your underwear all the way up and over your head."

For the next fifteen minutes, James laughed every time he imagined an atomic wedgy.

After hiking the barren ridge line for almost two hours—ascending several thousand feet above the river valley where they began—Sebastian and James came upon a suitable campsite for the night, which even included a little alpine pond surrounded by alder bushes. And though the summer sun was still fairly high, they set up camp for the night. Sebastian took several photographs of their tent with the mountain in the background, while James built a small campfire from dry alder twigs to boil pond water for their supper of dehydrated chili and macaroni noodles, which later proved to be a terrible choice for two people sleeping in the confines of a small tent.

From where the boys sat eating their warm meal in front of their little pitched tent, the mountain seemed close enough to touch.

"Dad would sure be impressed if he could see us now," James boasted while adding a handful of brittle twigs to the fire.

"I doubt it," replied Sebastian somberly. "He'd just say, 'A real man would already be halfway up the mountain! You sissies ain't nothin'!'"

SAVAGE MOUNTAIN

James nodded in agreement without looking up from the mesmerizing flames. "You sound just like him," he said with a kind of pathetic snicker followed by a long pensive silence.

BROTHERS
PILLAR OF THE COMMUNITY
APPLES & ORANGES
NOWHERE MAN
THE PLAN
DAY ONE
DAY TWO
DAY THREE
DAY FOUR
DAY FIVE
DAY SIX
DAY SEVEN
DAY EIGHT
THE RECKONING

Wednesday, July 2, 1980

IN ANY OTHER CORNER OF THE WORLD, at 5:47 a.m. one might say the boys awoke at sunrise. But during the brief Alaskan summer, the sun—even at a quarter to six—is always high in the sky.

Sebastian was the first to awaken.

He lay in his sleeping bag with his eyes closed, listening to occasional gusts blowing against the tent, bellowing the orange walls in and out as if it were alive and breathing. As he lay there feeling his muscles and shoulders already aching from the previous day's trek, he contemplated their planned route further up the mountainside. He could hear his brother snoring in the bag beside him. But he heard something else as well, a rustling and a strange snuffling sound. Sebastian opened his eyes and raised his head.

A grizzly bear was staring at him through the unzipped screen door, its moist nostrils flaring.

Sebastian screamed.

Startled, the bear turned its dark eyes, as big as tea saucers, and its short ears wriggled. James sat upright in his mummy bag, face-to-face with the bear. He screamed even louder than his brother, high pitched and bloodcurdling.

The frightened bear bolted.

The brothers scrambled out from the tent still in their underwear and jumped into the icy cold pond for safety. Both screamed again when they emerged from the bone-numbing water. They looked around for the bear. James spied it on a far hillside, still running, its blonde fur shining in the morning sun.

After changing into dry underwear, the boys lay in their sleeping bags for half an hour warming up. Sebastian heated water for instant oatmeal and coffee.

"Fine birthday this is turning out to be," said Sebastian.

"Oh, yeah! Today's your birthday. Happy birthday, Bro! Seventeen. Now you can see R-rated movies at the theatre."

"Big deal."

Neither said a word for a few minutes.

"Damn that pond is cold," said Sebastian. "Hey, remember the night that moose dragged us into the river?"

James chuckled just thinking about it.

"How could I forget? Dad always told us never to pitch our tent on a game trail, no matter how inviting it might seem."

"Yeah, but we did anyway."

"I remember it was late fall. Come nightfall that damn moose walked right through our camp, got all tangled up in our guy-lines, and dragged us down the trail, tent and all. I remember thinking it was an earthquake."

"I remember us laying inside our sleeping bags in pitch black wondering what the hell was going on."

"And then he dragged us down the steep bank and into the river," James continued. "Oh man, was that cold!"

"Hell, I thought we were going to drown. It seemed like forever before we got out of our bags and the tent and swam to shore."

James shook his head.

"I remember that was one miserable night, sitting there in the dark, soaking wet, shivering like crazy, waiting for daylight."

"When we told Dad about it all he said was, *I told you so, you dumbass kids.*"

Day Two

James ripped open two packages of instant oatmeal and poured them into his bowl.

"Yeah, that sounds like something he'd say," he said. "I remember another terrible night we spent in the woods."

"Oh, yeah? When was that?" Sebastian asked, while tearing open a brown packet.

"That bow hunting trip when we were tracking that wounded black bear."

"Oh, yeah, yeah. You missed your shot and just grazed the bear's shoulder. I remember following the blood trail until it started getting dark. Remember how it just stopped in the middle of that field all surrounded by dense brush and trees? That was weird."

"We had no idea which way the bear went,' interrupted James. "We didn't know if he was waiting to ambush us in the brush or if he had backtracked and was behind us. So we just stood in the darkness for hours listening to every sound, every rustling leaf, thinking the bear was creeping up on us."

"I remember wishing I had a rifle or a bazooka instead of a stupid bow," said Sebastian. "We were so cold and scared. But finally we made up our minds to go back the way we came and to run like hell, screaming as loud as we could. I was screaming my head off to scare the bear, which was easy 'cause I was really scared."

"Yeah, you sounded like when you're on a rollercoaster. Like an idiot."

"Hey, you're the one who missed his shot."

"We never told Mom and Dad about that night," said James. "They might never have let us go out again if they knew what happened on that trip, especially Mom. Dad would have been happy if the bear ate both of us."

"Probably."

They were quiet after that, thinking back to the bear in their tent.

"Oh, yeah," said James. "I forgot to tell you that you scream like a girl."

They laughed.

After breakfast, the boys dressed, brushed their teeth, packed up camp, refilled their canteens with water from the alpine pond, and started up the ridge again. They tied their wet underwear to the outside of their packs to dry. The going was steeper now, and the steep precipice to their right dropped thousands of feet into the green valley below.

An eagle soared below them, tipping its wings on an updraft.

By lunchtime, the boys had arrived at the pristine snowfields. For the most part, the rest of their adventure would be on snow and ice. They traded their leather hiking boots for their ungainly bunny boots. The going was slow in the sometimes waist-deep snow, deeper where the wind created drifts. The summer sun had created a thin crust on the surface of the snow that could almost bear their weight. But each time the crust would give way and they would sink into the snow, scrambling to get back onto the crust. It was hard going. They worked up a sweat just covering a few hundred yards. And although their packs felt heavy and cumbersome, in reality they were what climbing aficionados call *minimalists*. Unlike most Everest expeditions that hire as many as a dozen local Sherpa guides to carry the several tons of gear, including oxygen bottles, many of which must be transported and stockpiled near the Death Zone for the final summit push, the brothers carried everything they needed for the ascent by the sheer power of their own muscles, relying on no one else.

For the most part, mountaineers respect minimalists and traditionalists, but the larger mountains can take weeks, even months to climb, requiring much more gear and equipment, not to mention food, and therefore climbers require assistance to cart their gear to and up the mountain. Large mountains require a number of camps, staged at different altitudes, to serve as bases and to allow climbers time to acclimate to the thin air. Many cautious climbers have returned to the safety of a lower camp with the beckoning summit within reach. Those are the ones who live to climb another day.

Plodding along, struggling in the deep snow, stopping occasionally to catch their breath or to take drinks of water from their flasks, Sebastian and James carried their camp with them. The only time they planned to leave most of their equipment behind was for the final push to the summit. For that, they'd have to travel light and fast. Sebastian knew that the average stay on a summit was a matter of minutes.

Time was always of the essence.

All climbers know the saying, "What goes up, must come down." Sometimes the descent is more difficult and dangerous than the ascent. Many a climber's life has been lost on the way down, after using up every ounce of energy and resolve on the ascent.

The upward progress was exhausting.

For several hours the brothers moved by the sheer force of will, almost zombie-like at times, their minds mechanically thinking only about the next uphill step. Because the summer day was actually warm, neither wore his parka. Lost in their own thoughts, neither brother spoke as they trudged through the deep snow, taking turns to break trail up the increasingly steep slope.

"Let's take a break here," Sebastian said, as he shimmied the burdensome pack from his shoulders.

James removed his pack as well and dug out his water flask.

"This is tough-ass going," he said, wiping sweat from his eyes.

Sebastian looked up toward the white summit far above, wreathed by condensation. Its far remove seemed detached from their world, as if it were the peak of some distant mountain looming over another land, another world high above.

"Looks like it gets better from here on out. Looks like the wind has blown away a lot of the snow."

"I sure hope so," his tired brother replied.

Far below they could see the river and the place where the truck was parked. It looked like a gray speck. They could see the rivers and ponds and lakes and other mountain ranges in the distance, their peaks also shrouded in snow and ice, despite the green, rolling plateau and hills between them.

"Man, this is beautiful," Sebastian said with a gigantic smile. "I gotta get a picture."

He fished for his camera in the side pocket on his pack, snagged it, and took a picture of his brother. They stood side by side watching the picture develop.

"Perfect," said James when it was done. "Let me get one of you."

After rehydrating and snacking on a couple handfuls of trail mix—peanuts, M&Ms, raisins, and dried pineapple—the boys once again heaved their packs to their shoulders and resumed their ascent into the sky.

Far below, motorists and tourists driving along the highway, marveling at the mountain, had no idea that two teenage brothers were making their way, ant-like, up the frozen slope. Just as the peak seemed remote from their world, so Sebastian and James felt as if they were the only two people in the world.

Late in the day, they arrived at the edge of Sanford Glacier. Gusts blowing off the glacier had scoured away much of the snow, leaving a patch of barren ground.

"We have to cross here," said Sebastian, remembering the route up the North Ramp he had marked out on the laminated map inside his parka pocket.

James surveyed the wide glacier with its many crevasses like open mouths waiting to swallow. From experience, he knew that many lay concealed beneath a thin mantle of snow.

He gulped hard.

"It's time for supper," Sebastian continued. "Let's set up camp here for the night and hit it in the morning."

Day Two

James nodded in agreement, glad for the news. Nowhere near as athletic as Sebastian, he was dog-dead tired. The deep snow had really taken its toll.

Although they moved slowly, especially James, the boys cleared a fairly level area of rocks and set up their small tent, piling rocks atop the stakes to keep the tent from blowing away should the wind kick up. After settling down inside the fluttering tent, Sebastian cooked dinner over the little stove. The dehydrated turkey tetrazzini was surprisingly delicious, but the two reconstituted hamburger patties tasted like wooden hockey pucks.

After dinner, Sebastian lay in his green Army surplus sleeping bag reading a slender edition of *Hamlet*, the only book he had brought on the journey. James lay in his bag playing a slow, sad song on his harmonica. Suddenly he stopped playing and was quiet for a moment, just lying in his bag staring at the low ceiling trembling in the wind.

"Why do you think Dad hates us so much?" he finally said. "I mean . . . do you think he wishes we didn't even exist?"

The abrupt question startled Sebastian, who paused before answering.

"Get some sleep. We got a hard climb tomorrow."

Sebastian dog-eared the page he was reading, put down the book, and turned over onto his side, facing away from his brother, signaling that the conversation was over.

For a few minutes James lay staring at the tent ceiling.

Finally, he zipped his green mummy bag up to his neck so that only the small circle of his face showed. Shortly afterwards, both boys were snoring. Several times during the night, the fracturing glacier awoke the brothers from their restless sleep.

Thursday, July 3, 1980

THE NEXT MORNING WAS CLOUDIER than the previous day. Ten thousand feet above the flapping tent a long, grayish cloud raked the summit, and spindrift blew off a knife-sharp ridge line, indicating high winds. More clouds gathered on the horizon. With a cup of hot coffee in his bare hands, Sebastian surveyed the glacier between him and the North Ramp, squinting from the blinding whiteness.

James crawled out from the tent, stretched and yawned. His hair was messed up royally.

"So, what's the plan?" he asked, scratching his head.

"I think we need to follow this ridge a little higher and cross there," said Sebastian, pointing to a spot several hundred yards above their camp. "It looks safer there."

"Whatever you say, Bro," replied James, taking a few steps away from camp and turning his back to his brother to urinate on the rocks.

Sebastian did the same thing, first setting his coffee cup on a flat rock.

"Let's eat something and hit the road," he said a minute later, zipping up his pants.

After dismantling the tent and meticulously packing all their

85

equipment—rolling their sleeping bags tightly—the brothers worked their way up the mountain to begin their trek across the glacier at the point where Sebastian had suggested. From where they stood on the rocky ridge, the way across looked only a fraction less dangerous than any other place on the glacier. Crevasses appeared where the ice had fractured. Some were wide and hundreds of feet deep. While the surface of the glacier looked mostly white, the chasms looked bluish inside from sunlight trying to penetrate the dense ice.

"I think we should long-rope our way across, just in case," said Sebastian, taking off his pack and pulling out a 150-foot-long coil of green and red climbing rope. "Time to dig out our crampons."

The brothers cinched their crampons over the soles of their white boots, making sure the straps were tight. The sharp metal teeth would bite into the glacial ice, giving them traction. For the most part, a person can walk on a glacier in tennis shoes. Specks of airborne dust and tiny rocks become embedded into the surface of the glacier in the slight melt under the summer sun, creating a rough, porous, almost sandpaper-like surface. Every summer, thousands of tourists explore the terminus and end moraines of popular, easy-access glaciers, like Matanuska Glacier or Exit Glacier. But one wrong step and a person can disappear forever.

With a slight shiver, the brothers recalled what had happened to a young boy on a glacier about eighty miles east of Anchorage a couple years earlier. Stories about it had circulated in the news for days.

The twelve-year-old boy was part of a Boy Scout troop exploring Matanuska Glacier. He was walking alongside a meltwater chute—a shallow stream carved on the surface of a glacier—when he fell in. At first it was almost funny as he slid slowly along in the slick chute, almost like a water-park amusement ride. Two boys ran alongside him laughing and heckling. But,

Day Three

ahead, around a bend in the ice, the flow picked up speed, dramatically, and the rivulet poured into a moulin, a hole drilled into the ice by the warmer, rushing water. Moulins are narrow, twisting tunnels bored through the glacier, sometimes for thousands of feet, even longer, sometimes constricting, sometimes opening up. Many reach all the way down through the darkness to the bedrock, lubricating the belly of the slow-moving glacier.

When the scouts running alongside the chute saw the gaping maw of the moulin, they shouted to their friend to get out, frantically holding out their hands, trying to grab his. But it was no use. The walls of the chute were polished smooth and slick. As his friends watched in horror, the frightened boy slipped into the hole and was gone. Rescuers later lowered a waterproof video-camera down the hole for hundreds of feet until they ran out of rope, but they never found him.

Sebastian and James shuddered at the thought of the boy's corpse still down there, porcelain white, frozen solid—a part of the creeping glacier—the thunderous rush of meltwater cascading over him.

James had almost fallen into a moulin once. He and Sebastian were hunting mountain sheep the previous fall when they crossed a small glacier to get to a band of sheep they had seen on the other side of the steep valley. James slipped into a chute and was sliding toward the hole, which was about three feet across. In a moment of desperation, Sebastian extended the butt of his rifle, and James latched on.

It was a close call. One of many.

Death is like that in Alaska—always and unexpectedly waiting around the corner.

For safety's sake, the brothers both tied an end of the rope around their waist. They would take turns leading. If one brother fell into a crevasse, the other would be able to pull him out. In some expeditions, entire teams are sometimes connected by a single rope, especially in whiteout conditions, when visibility is reduced to several feet. Of course, the danger with long-roping is that if one climber falls the entire team is endangered.

It had happened many times.

Sebastian led the way across the glacier with his ice ax in his hand. James followed a hundred feet behind, with his ice ax also at the ready. Halfway across, Sebastian came upon a crevasse, which was about ten feet across with no way around it. He stopped and waited for his brother.

"Think we can jump to the other side?" he asked.

James peered over the edge. The crevasse looked fifty or sixty feet deep, the icy, blue-tinted walls nearly vertical and narrowing toward its yawning depth.

"No way," he replied, nervously backing away from the edge. "Maybe in gym class wearing shorts and sneakers, but I'm not gonna try."

Sebastian pretended to push his brother closer to the edge. Startled, James just about jumped out of his boots in fear.

"I was just pulling your leg." Sebastian laughed. "I wasn't going to jump either. Let's find a way around it."

Leading the way again, with the hundred feet of rope connecting them, Sebastian worked his way across the glacier, staying far from the gaping crevasse. Suddenly there was a loud crack. Sebastian froze instantly. They both knew the sound. Sebastian was standing on top of a crevasse, only a thin layer of crusted snow between him and the frozen depths.

"Don't move!" James shouted.

"What do you think I'm doing?" Sebastian yelled back, his tone sarcastic but full of fear.

"Hold on," replied James, stamping his feet hard on the glacier, one foot in front of the other, so that the crampon spikes dug deep into the ice.

"Okay!" he shouted when he felt his foothold was solid. "Walk back toward me! Slowly!"

Sebastian took one cautious backward step.

Day Three

The surface of the glacier complained with a loud pop.

James pulled in the slack.

Sebastian took another step, sliding one foot ahead of the other, the way people check for thin ice on a frozen pond.

The glacier complained again, even louder.

James pulled in the slack again and hunkered down a bit, readying himself.

"Steady," he shouted.

Sebastian took another step. This time the crusted snow gave way and Sebastian plummeted into the chasm. The sudden force yanked James to his stomach and dragged him across the surface of the glacier toward the edge. He drove his ax pick into the ice in a maneuver called a self-arrest, the sudden anchor swinging his body around violently to a stop. With the pick planted into the surface of the glacier, James clambered to his feet, planting his crampon spikes into the ice so he could bear the weight of his brother.

"You alright?" he shouted.

"I'm okay!" Sebastian shouted back, his words muffled from inside the crevasse. "Get me outta here!"

"Hang in there," replied James. "I got you."

James pulled the rope, hand over hand, foot by foot, drawing his brother from the abyss. Finally, an ice ax arced from the hole and stabbed into the ice, and was followed by Sebastian's grimacing face. A moment later, after scrambling over the edge, Sebastian was lying on his back atop the glacier, several feet clear of the crevasse.

"Oh man, that was close!" he said. "I'd have been a goner without you."

"Good thing we were roped in," replied James, extending a hand to help his brother to his feet.

After catching their breath and calming their nerves, the boys descended a hundred yards below the crevasse before continuing their trek across the glacier, avoiding a moulin they encountered on the way. An hour later they were once again standing on terra firma. Behind them was the perilous glacier; before them was a 500-foot free fall. Above them was an ominous ridge line that ran nearly 2,000 feet.

Sebastian started stacking a pile of rocks.

"What's that for?" asked James.

"So we remember to cross here on the way back."

While Sebastian made the marker, James took out a baggie of marijuana from inside his parka, rolled a fatty, and lit it.

Sebastian smelled the smoke and stopped what he was doing.

"Is that what I think it is?" he asked.

"Yeah," replied James. "I brought some Mary Jane. Want some?"

"Sure," Sebastian replied with a disarming smile, reaching out to take a hit.

James handed over the dooby after a long drag.

Instantly, Sebastian snatched the plastic sandwich bag from his brother's hand and tossed it over the cliff face, flicking the joint over as well.

"What the hell are you doing, man?" shouted James, exhaling a cloud of smoke and shoving Sebastian. "That weed cost me thirty bucks!"

Sebastian shoved back.

"No drugs. You're staying clean on this trip," replied Sebastian.

James shoved Sebastian so hard Sebastian fell off the rocky outcropping onto the glacier.

"You're not the boss of me!" he barked.

"You're not getting high on this trip!" Sebastian yelled, getting onto his knees.

"Get off my case!" James shouted, jumping down and standing over his brother with both fists clinched.

Still kneeling on the ice, Sebastian grabbed James's feet and pulled them out from beneath him. James fell over, and they wrestled on the glacier, rolling around, each trying to get atop the other to punch him in the face.

Finally, Sebastian got his brother in a headlock.

Day Three

"You gonna stop?" he shouted, tightening his grip so James could barely breathe.

James struggled to escape, but Sebastian's grip was too strong. Finally, he relaxed and lay still on the cold, hard ice.

"I . . . give," he croaked.

Sebastian let go of James and they both stood up, wiping snow from their clothes and each eyeing the other suspiciously. Sebastian returned to look for more rocks to place on the marker. James stood looking over the cliff for his baggie of pot, an updraft blowing his hair into his face.

"Man, that ain't right . . . throwing away perfectly good weed."

He was mad at his brother, but he also accepted that the dangers of climbing required clear thinking, steady hands, and fast reflexes. The incident with the crevasse was a perfect reminder of the impending dangers.

"Let's take a breather and make some coffee," said Sebastian, removing his back pack and digging out the little camp stove and pot. "Besides, I think I have to take a dump after getting the crap scared out of me."

James chuckled.

While the water heated, they sat on rocks facing the glacier they had just crossed.

"Remember when we were kids sitting around the campfire and Uncle Herb told us those stories about the giant ice worms that live on glaciers?" asked James.

"Yeah. I remember. And I thought the stories were true," replied Sebastian.

"Me too. I thought they were like a hundred feet long and ate caribou and mountain sheep."

"When I got older I didn't believe in them anymore," said Sebastian, "until we started exploring glaciers on our own and learned that the worms really do exist, only they're tiny—like an inch long—living in the ice, coming to the surface to eat pollen blown onto the glaciers from surrounding hillsides."

91

"Goes to show you that myths and legends like that aren't true," said James.

"I've been thinking about that," replied Sebastian. "I think it means that myths have some grain of truth to them, only parts of the story get exaggerated over time," replied Sebastian.

"Kind of like that gossip game where one person tells another person something and that person tells the next and so on until, by the time it gets to the fifth or sixth person, it's not even the same thing anymore."

"Yeah, sort of," replied Sebastian.

When the water came to a near boil, Sebastian poured two cups of instant coffee, handing one to his brother.

"Thanks," said James, after taking a sip. "I'm still pissed about the weed."

"So sue me," replied Sebastian with a broad smile, cupping his hands around the hot metal cup.

After the break, they resumed their ascent, climbing up the steep ridge drifted with deep snow and with dangerous overhangs that could unexpectedly break away, sending them careening thousands of feet over the edge. For safety's sake, the boys were again connected by 150 feet of rope. At the higher altitude, the temperature dropped and the wind increased. Sudden gusts threatened to sweep them from the mountain. Both boys wore their goggles to protect their eyes and had their thick hoods pulled up. It took several hours to climb a vertical distance that a person could have walked horizontally in a matter of minutes. To make matters worse, a dense cloud bank was blowing in from the north, bringing with it the possibility of a blizzard.

More than once they grumbled, questioning what they were doing. Their friends were all back in town where the temperature was in the 80s. They were sleeping late, watching television, listening to records, going to movies, and hanging out together at the mall. They were mowing lawns, washing cars, riding bikes, working temporary summer jobs, and swimming and suntanning at local lakes.

Their friends were taking it easy, enjoying summer vacation.

But Sebastian and James trudged on, for reasons neither cared to try to put into shared words, forcing their way upward, hell-bent on getting to the top, in some way proving their worth to their father. Both were exhausted. Sebastian thought about the line where Hamlet says, "To sleep, perchance to dream." While he understood that Hamlet was contemplating the nature of death, Sebastian just wished he was home asleep in his nice, warm bed dreaming of distant mountains.

He thought about something else as well.

Looking down at the world more than 10,000 feet below, he knew there would be no rescue in the event of an emergency. In their secrecy, neither he nor his brother had told a living soul where they were really going. If something happened to them, no one would come looking for them on the mountain. Other climbers would one day find their frozen corpses half buried on the snowy slopes, resolving the mystery of their disappearance, but that might be years hence.

For an instant, the true nature of their predicament made Sebastian sick to his stomach.

Maybe climbing the mountain wasn't such a good idea after all, he thought.

At about 12,000 feet, they called it a day and set up their tent on the only flat spot they could find, a precarious ledge about nine feet wide by fifteen or sixteen feet long with a 3,000-foot free fall below. They secured the tent's guy-lines to pitons hammered into the cliff face, so the tent wouldn't blow off the ledge with them inside. Climbers call such a precarious perch on a mountainside a bivouac. They were both exhausted, unused to the physical demands of climbing a high mountain in deep snow with a wind blasting in their faces. No amount of training prepares climbers for the actual rigors encountered once on the mountain, though it certainly doesn't hurt to stay in shape. Climbers frequently lose significant weight on expeditions, returning home gaunt as ghosts.

After a dinner of reconstituted chicken teriyaki with rice, Sebastian examined both pairs of crampons, checking the leather straps for damage and sharpening any spikes that had dulled. He knew it was imperative to take care of their equipment.

Their lives depended on it.

Later, once again lying inside their green sleeping bags on their blue pads, James played his harmonica while Sebastian was rereading the soliloquy where Hamlet asks himself the famous question, "To be, or not to be?" The play really spoke to Sebastian, who was only a few years younger than was Hamlet and equally confused. He didn't know any better than Hamlet what to do. He didn't know what course of action he should take. He felt as if no one in the world would understand what he was going through. He was often overwhelmed with a sense of being alone.

Just like Hamlet.

Sebastian folded the corner of the page he was reading and settled the book across his chest.

"I don't know why he hates us so much," he said casually to the tent ceiling.

"What?" asked James, stopping mid-song.

"Your question last night . . . about Dad . . . about why he hates us."

Neither brother said anything for a long minute. James played a few depressing notes on his harmonica and then stopped.

"Which one of us do you think he hates the most?" he asked.

"That's a dumb question. He hates us both."

"I think he hates you more because you were the one who first ruined his life," said James matter-of-factly. "You made him a prisoner by having to get married young because Mom was pregnant with you. Maybe he had other dreams for his life and you took them away."

Day Three

James remembered the afternoon when he'd came home and heard his father shouting and breaking all his trophies.

"He really hates you for that. Maybe he sees how bright your future is going to be and he resents you for it. You keep trying to impress him, like climbing this stupid mountain, but all you do is make him hate you more. I bet he wishes you were never born."

"Shut up! Shut up!" Sebastian shouted, violently shaking his fist inches from his brother's face, as if he wanted to punch him in the mouth to stop him from talking. "He hates you more! You're nothing but a loser! You're the one he wishes didn't exist!"

Sebastian went outside and sat on the ledge, his feet dangling in space. He could hear his brother sobbing inside the tent.

For a long time Sebastian watched the sun creeping low on the horizon. He looked at the wide, green plateau far below where they had begun their ascent of the mountain by fording the river. He looked at the summit above, almost a vertical mile away, feeling as if his whole life was like this predicament: caught in between something insurmountable—between a rock and a hard place.

How easy it would be just to slide off this ledge and end everything, he thought.

But he didn't do it. He wouldn't leave his brother to face the mountain alone. He wouldn't leave him to face their father alone either.

When Sebastian finally crawled back into the tent, James was curled up on his side asleep.

Independence Day, July 4, 1980

THE TENT WALLS WERE FLAILING HARD when the boys awoke. They took their time getting up, their muscles stiff and sore. Both had headaches from mild dehydration. After a leisurely breakfast of pancakes, powdered eggs, and instant coffee, Sebastian got dressed and crawled out from the tent and stretched.

He stood on the ledge and surveyed the world.

The cloud cover seemed denser than it had been the day before. Sebastian studied their ascent route, which looked less perilous than the knife-sharp ridge they had climbed the day before. The snowy slope was steep, but not technical, meaning that it could be climbed without establishing a main line with pitons. He couldn't see what lay above the slope, but he knew from the map that they'd be within a couple thousand feet of the summit once they got beyond whatever lay hidden from view. His only concern was the snow load, which looked heavy. He could see an overhang at the top and where little avalanches had already slid down the chutes and runnels, natural gullies that channeled avalanches like a riverbed.

James crawled out from the tent and stood beside his brother on the narrow ledge, looking at the perilous 3,000-foot drop.

"The first step's a doozy," he joked.

"That's for sure," replied Sebastian.

"Whew! Chilly," said James, pulling on his wool cap over his ears.

"Where do we go from here?" he asked.

"I think we can summit today. We'll work our way over there, around that snow chute, and then cross over to there," replied Sebastian, tracing their proposed route in the air with his index finger. "Once we make it above this slope, we should be able to reach the summit in an hour or two."

"We gonna pack up camp?" asked James.

"No. We'll leave it here. We should be able to make summit and climb back down just in time for dinner, with maybe an hour or two to spare. We'll travel light and fast, carrying our packs with just our climbing gear and some quick-energy snacks."

"Speaking of lightening the load," said James, unzipping his pants and whizzing over the edge, the stream of pee traveling over half a mile to the bottom of the cliff.

Sebastian joined him.

"Hey," he said with a grin. "I bet we're setting a world record for the longest pee."

James laughed.

Leaving the tent set up with the sleeping bags, pads, cooking stove and pot, stainless-steel dishes and utensils, food, and extra clothes inside, they struck out for the summit. They used their ice axes to help as they made their way up the slope through deep snow. Once again, a rope connected the brothers, who stopped often to catch their breath, leaning over their ice axes, beholding the amazing scene below. At almost 14,000 feet, they were above the neighboring mountains as well as the clouds on the horizon.

The view was spectacular, but time was too short to spend in sightseeing.

Suddenly, a loud rumble bellowed from above. They looked up just in time to see a wall of snow coming at them down the chute.

"Use your ax!" Sebastian shouted, dropping to his knees and

planting his ice ax into the snow and hanging on for dear life.

James managed to use his ax just in time.

But their actions were futile against the wall of snow thundering toward them. The avalanche engulfed them, tumbling them head over heels down the high ridge for a thousand feet. Sebastian still gripped his ice ax, but it was worse than useless, more likely to impale him than to aid him. When he finally came to rest, he was only partially buried. He had lost his wool cap and one of his gloves. After pulling himself out of the compacted snow, he looked around and discovered he was only a couple hundred feet from the edge of the precipice. Then he looked for his brother. James was nowhere to be seen on the jumbled field of snow.

"James! James!" he yelled in a dizzy panic, frantically looking in every direction and digging snow out from his ears and nose.

Sebastian felt for the rope around his waist. It was still tied securely, which meant that his brother might still be on the other end. He grabbed the rope and began to yank. As each foot of the rope emerged from the snow, he followed it. In some places the rope was buried a couple feet deep and Sebastian had to yank hard to pull it out.

Occasionally he'd stop, shout for his brother, and blow the shrill whistle hanging from his parka zipper. But he heard nothing except the wind. Sebastian knew that with every passing minute his brother, buried somewhere in the haphazard snowfield, could be freezing to death, or worse, suffocating.

Feverishly, Sebastian yanked out the rope until finally, sixty feet from where he had pulled himself free, he felt the weight of his brother beneath him. He quickly removed the shovel from his pack and began to dig his brother out.

"I'm here! Hold on!" he screamed as he dug, careful not to strike his brother with the sharp blade of the shovel.

While digging, Sebastian wondered what he would tell his parents if he didn't come home with his brother. How would he tell them that his frozen corpse was buried somewhere on the side of a mountain?

Finally, almost three feet deep, Sebastian saw the red of his brother's parka. Using his bare hands, he kept digging until he was able to pull James upright, his lower body still buried. James opened his eyes.

"Wha . . . what . . . to-took . . . you . . . s-so . . . long?" he said through chattering teeth.

Wrapping his arms beneath both armpits, Sebastian pulled James out from the snowy grave. He had lost both of his gloves, his cap, and his ice ax. His parka hood was packed with snow, and the force of the avalanche had pulled his snow pants down around his ankles, kept on only by the bulky bunny boots. His blue jeans were soaking wet.

James was shivering uncontrollably.

Sebastian had to get his brother back to their tent quickly if he were going to save him. He knew the dangers of hypothermia. A year before, he and James had spent a week enduring an Arctic survival training course during January, the coldest time of the year. Temperatures reached fifty below zero for much of the week. The instructors had shown movies about the effects of hypothermia, replete with footage of people whose hands or feet, nose or ears were so frozen that they would have to be amputated. Sebastian remembered vividly the images of grotesquely swollen black toes and fingers, called *blebs*. One of the first symptoms of hypothermia is disorientation and the inability to speak clearly or to make sense. The incapacity to think rationally is also symptomatic of the onset of hypothermia, as the body begins to freeze from the outside inward. Shivering is one of the body's only defenses. But it's a feeble defense against such bone-cracking cold. In its attempt to save the brain and the heart, the body shuts down everything that is not vital to survival.

The history of mountaineering is littered with tales of hypothermic victims, many of whom have been found frozen to death with much of their clothing removed, as if they were overheating. The truth is they were so cold that their body no longer felt anything, and they misinterpreted the lack of sensation as meaning they no longer needing their coats and hats and gloves. In their delirium, many victims have simply walked off the side of a mountain into oblivion. Some report having suffered bizarre hallucinations. Many climbers who have lost a finger, a toe, or a bit of an ear to frostbite wear their wounds like a badge of honor, proof of their near-death experience and tenacity in the face of extreme hardship and peril.

A few years earlier, while snowmobiling on a cold day, Sebastian had suffered frostbite on the skin between his eyebrows and the bridge of his nose. The skin had never fully healed and never would.

Fearing for his brother's life, Sebastian acted quickly.

He pulled up his brother's snow pants, brushed the snow away from inside his parka hood and pulled it over his brother's head, making sure it was on securely. He rooted through both packs for extra gloves. The whole time he spoke to James to keep him awake.

"Stay with me," he said, gently slapping his brother's red cheeks. "I'm gonna get you back to camp. You're gonna be alright."

Then he lifted James to his feet, steadying him until he could balance on his own.

Sebastian tied one end of a short piece of rope around his brother's waist and the other around his own. Mustering all his strength, he short-roped his brother, leading the way and pulling James whenever he lagged behind, trying to coax him back to camp. Sometimes he had to fall back and half carry him. On several occasions, James lost his balance, fell facedown into the snow and lay there, not even trying to get up.

"Get up! You gotta help me!" Sebastian shouted above the wind while standing over his brother.

"I just wanna sleep here for a while," James replied wearily, his voice raspy.

"You can't sleep now," said Sebastian, struggling to pull James to his feet. "I can't carry you. You have to walk. Get up!"

It took almost an hour for the two to get back to their tent on the precarious ledge. Once inside, Sebastian stripped James of his boots and crampons and wet clothes and helped him into his sleeping bag, placing his own bag on top for added warmth. He heated water for hot tea to warm their insides. The cooking stove warmed the small tent, but Sebastian knew he couldn't let it burn for too long. The carbon monoxide fumes could kill them just as surely as the cold.

James slept for several hours while Sebastian read his book, stopping frequently to check on his brother. More and more, he sympathized with Hamlet's circumstance. Who could he talk to? Who could he trust? What power did he have, if any, to change the way things were? And worse of all: Was death the only escape?

Finally, James opened his eyes and sighed.

"What happened?" he asked, looking around, confused.

"We got caught in an avalanche. You were buried for half an hour before I found you."

"I remember seeing the avalanche coming at me," said James, licking his dry lips. "I vaguely remember waking up and realizing that I was buried. I couldn't move at all. It was like I was in cement. I remember thinking I was going to die."

"Well, you didn't, Bro, not yet," Sebastian said with a smile.

"Now we're even," said James. "I saved your life and you saved mine."

James pulled his hands out from the sleeping bag and studied them, wiggling his fingers and balling his fists.

"They're okay," said Sebastian, understanding his brother's concern. "I got you back here in the nick of time."

James put his hands back inside the warm sleeping bag.

Day Four

"So, what do we do now?"

"I don't know," replied Sebastian, looking at his wristwatch. "You're in no shape to climb right now, and, besides, it's too late to make another summit attempt today. Besides, we need to decide if we even want to keep on going."

"Because of me?" asked James.

Sebastian nodded but added, "That too."

"I feel okay. A bit tired still."

"But why should we go on at all?" Sebastian asked while he poured a cup of hot tea and handed it to his brother. "I mean, what are we risking our lives for? We both could have died. Maybe next time we won't be so lucky. We could just head back down and go home."

James took a long drink of tea before responding.

"Because of Dad," he said, wiping his mouth with the back of his hand. "Because we *need* to."

Neither brother spoke for a minute. Outside, the wind was raging. Sebastian worried the pitons might come loose or the guy-lines snap, sending the tent right off the mountain.

"Just for once, I wish he'd be proud of us, you know what I mean?" Sebastian said loud enough to be heard above the machine-gun rattle of the tent walls flapping in the barbarous wind. "I've done everything to make him proud of me, and I don't even know why. He's a jerk. Why should I care? Why am I risking my life to prove something to him?"

"Because he's our father," replied James.

"Yeah," Sebastian said softly, looking down at the tent floor strewn with packs and clothes and gear.

"So, what are we gonna do?" asked James, trying to rally his brother. "Let the bastard win or show him what we're made of? We're more men than that bastard any day."

Sebastian was impressed by his brother's enthusiasm, especially after surviving the avalanche. "I say we keep going. Let's eat, hydrate, get a good night's sleep, and boogie up this mother in the morning—that is, if this wind lets up," he said, listening to the tempest outside. "What do you want for dinner: dehydrated Chili Mac or Top Ramen?" he asked, holding up two packets.

"I vote for noodles," said James, remembering what happened after eating chili the last time.

Saturday, July 5, 1980

THE SUMMIT BECKONED as the boys, on hands and knees in their red long johns, peeked out the fly of their tent. The wind had died down overnight, and most of the clouds were gone. It was a perfect day for a summit attempt.

Within an hour, Sebastian and James were once again climbing the steep snowy slope, connected by rope. With his ice ax in hand, Sebastian led the way. The going was easier than the day before. They no longer worried about an avalanche, and the snow was packed all the way up the slide area where the avalanche had thundered down the side of the mountain.

They made good time.

Without incident, the brothers surmounted the crest and stood side by side marveling at the peak towering above them, maybe only 1,500 feet away. But between them was an eighty-five-foot cliff face, as tall and steep as an eight-story building. There was a difficult outcrop near the top. Above that was a treacherous snow-covered ridge line with angular cornices leading up to the summit. The cliff offered no way around. It reminded Sebastian of the Hillary Step at the top of Everest, which he had only read about and seen in books. They would have to manage a technical climb, setting pitons into the rock to secure the rope up the rock face. Without saying a word, they pulled off their backpacks and dug out the gear they would need, including their bandoleers of carabineers and pitons, as well as their piton hammers and helmets. They both took out a piece of green rope about eight feet long and tied a seat harness, running the rope around their waist and between their legs at the crotch, making a classic climbing harness. They double-checked that their harnesses and knots were tight.

"I'll lead the pitch," said Sebastian, using jargon that meant he would lead the way up a cliff and "fix" the route.

Recognizing that his brother was the stronger climber between them, James didn't argue the point.

"Be my guest," he said, gesturing his brother to go on ahead.

Sebastian tied the sharp end of the rope, as climbers say, to a carabineer—adding an extra half-hitch knot for safety—and clipped it to the front of his harness. Methodically, he worked his way up the rock, looking for hand- and footholds, and stopping every so often to drive a piton or a wafer into a crack in the rock face with his hammer. When he was certain the piton was secure, Sebastian connected a carabineer to the piton eyelet and clipped the rope in so that, should he slip, the piton would arrest his fall. It was his brother's job to pull any slack out of the rope, but not so taut that Sebastian couldn't climb unrestrained. For mountain climbers, there is no past or future. There is only the present, only the intense awareness of finding the next safe hold, and the insatiable desire to reach the blue-edged horizon.

From below, with the rope sliding along his lower back and gripped in his leather-gloved hands, James steadily paid out rope, keenly watching every move his brother made, ready in an instant to brake the line across his chest should his brother lose his hand- or foothold.

James could hear the steady *tink-tink-tink* of pitons ringing home as Sebastian pounded them into solid rock. Experienced climbers can recognize the sound of brittle, rotten rock. Every now and then a hail of small stones rained down on him from above.

"Rock!" Sebastian shouted, as a fist-sized rock broke loose and fell close to James.

"Hey! Be careful up there!" James yelled. "You trying to kill me?"

"Sorry!" Sebastian replied, without taking his eyes off what he was doing.

Sebastian angled up and across the rock face, looking for his best route. Halfway up, he came upon a chimney, a split in the rock about three feet across and about thirty feet tall. Most climbers, especially freestyle climbers, like chimneys because they can use the close walls in ways they can't when scaling a face. In the narrow confines of a chimney, climbers can use opposing pressures to shimmy upward—a hand pressing against one side with the back and a knee offering opposing pressure. Generally, alpinists avoid using knees altogether. Their round nature is dodgy.

After an hour of strenuous climbing, Sebastian scrambled over the top of the overhang and unclipped his carabineer from the rope.

"Off belay!" he shouted down to his brother, letting him know that he was no longer on the rope.

No longer responsible for his brother's life, James relaxed his stance and wiped snot from his nose, which had been bothering him, dripping into his mouth.

Sebastian quickly secured himself with a piton, tested it, dug out his black leather gloves, and tossed over a rope so he could help pull his brother to the top.

James tied the end of the rope to a carabineer, which he clipped to his harness. Taking no chances, he also tied an extra half-hitch.

"On belay," James yelled, informing Sebastian that his life was now in his brother's hands.

With the added safety of the rope, James made his way quickly to the top. The brothers took a short break to drink some water, conceding one of the fundamental tenets in climbing: *hydrate, hydrate, hydrate.* They also ate a couple handfuls of trail mix. While they rested, they studied the last stage up the mountain.

"What a sight," said James. "If Dad could only see us now."

"Who gives a damn what he thinks?" replied Sebastian, standing up and sliding his plastic flask back into the inside pocket of his parka.

"We'll long-rope the rest of the way, just to be safe," he said. "Let's get at it."

The last leg to the summit was easy compared to other parts of the ascent. The snow was hard-packed, so the teeth of their crampons made the boys as sure-footed as mountain sheep. And although the steepness made the going laborious, along with an increasing need to pause to breathe in the thinning air, enthusiasm at being so close to their goal spurred the brothers onward. So high up, the wind was fierce. They had to wear their ski goggles to protect their eyes.

By early afternoon, Sebastian and James stood on the pyramid-shaped peak, 16,237 feet above sea level, congratulating each another, shaking hands, and slapping each other on the back. They snapped a few photographs to prove their achievement. If you've never stood on the top of a great mountain, the only way to appreciate the accomplishment is to look out the window of a jet airliner as it climbs to altitude, and note how small the world below appears as the plane approaches 20,000 feet.

The view is oddly beautiful and terrifying at the same time.

The mountain's reward is only granted—begrudgingly—to those who have toiled and suffered and earned the right. The gift is profound awareness of timelessness and eternity and an unobstructed beauty that no climber ever forgets. No matter how many years pass, the memory persists. It is, perhaps, that haunting and undiminished recollection that beckons the mountaineer again and again to high places.

Climbers spend so much time and effort to reach the summit,

to linger for mere minutes. The feeling of joy intermingles with a sense of dread. Looking down at the distance they have traveled and at the obstacles they have overcome—sometimes by the grace of God and often at the cost of a fellow climber's life—all climbers know they must descend. Almost always exhausted by the time they summit, many lack the willpower and dogged determination that spurred them on to the top. Because of this, most mountaineering accidents happen on the way down.

Noticing that a sinister cold front was blowing in from the north, darkening the summer sky, the brothers took one last look at the 360-degree panoramic view, and committing it to memory for the rest of their lives, they began their descent. They safely long-lined down the snow-laden ridge with its projecting cornices; they rappelled safely down the eighty-five-foot cliff with its cleft chimney, like a deep scar in the face of the rock; and they made it safely down the slope where James had been buried alive the day before.

By the time they arrived at their tent, Sebastian and James were famished, having burned up far more calories than they had consumed at breakfast. They were not only seriously hungry but thirsty and exhausted as well. Their knees ached from the downhill trek. But they were also exhilarated from having achieved what they had set out to do.

The tent warmed as Sebastian heated water to reconstitute their dehydrated dinner.

"What is this?" James asked when his brother handed him a steaming plate.

"Chicken á la king."

James took a bite, grimacing as he swallowed.

"Oh man, that's bad. They should call it 'chicken á la crap.'"

"Hey, don't blame me. I just added hot water according to the instructions. Besides, it's not that bad," replied Sebastian, taking a bite.

"If you say so," said James, choking down another sporkful. "Yuck!"

"I'm sorry your sophisticated palate disapproves," remarked Sebastian snidely. "I'll have the bellhop send up something more to your liking, escargot or caviar, perhaps. Or maybe we could just get a Big Mac at that McDonald's I saw halfway down the last cliff?"

"Hilarious," replied James. "Don't count on a tip. The service here sucks."

After dinner, the brothers played poker with a deck of cards that James had brought along in his pack.

"Gimme two," he said, laying two cards face down.

Sebastian handed him two cards off the top of the deck.

James grinned as he laid out his hand.

"Three Jacks. Read 'em and weep, Loser," he gloated.

Sebastian revealed his cards.

"A pair of fours. You win."

James sniffed the air and cringed.

"No! Not again!" he groaned, closing his eyes as if they were stinging.

A smile grew across Sebastian's face.

"I can't help it," he apologized. "It's that damn chicken."

James wrinkled his nose and winced. "Gross!"

"He who smelt it dealt it," replied Sebastian with a dark chuckle.

James opened the tent fly and fanned the air, as if trying to blow the odor out the door.

"Oh, man that's gnarly!" he said. "Sick! What crawled up your butt and died?"

Covering his mouth and nose with his sweater, James spoke through the makeshift gas mask.

"Seriously! You need to see a doctor! Oh! That's just wrong!"

As a crisp breeze refreshed their tent, the boys resumed their card game. A little later, while watching his brother intently scrutinizing his hand, Sebastian chose the cozy moment to bring up something he wanted to talk about.

Day Five

"Hey, James?"

"Hmm?" James murmured without looking up.

"I'm sorry about what I said the other day . . . about you being a loser."

James looked up from his cards.

"I wasn't really mad at you," Sebastian continued. "I'm . . . I am mad at Dad, at the whole friggin' situation. What you said really got to me. I just couldn't take another word."

James pulled a card from his hand and set it face down.

"One," he said.

Sebastian handed his brother a new card. James picked it up and frowned looking at it.

"I'm sorry about what I said about Dad hating you most, about you ruining his life," he said. "I was wrong."

"No . . . the more I think about it the more I think you're right."

"I know it must have been hard for you to hear," James said.

Sebastian discarded one card and drew a new one. He smiled.

"Full house," he bragged, laying down his fanned-out cards. "Queens over nines. Let's see ya beat that."

"I got nothing," replied James, showing his losing hand.

Sebastian set the deck aside. His expression turned serious.

"I heard you crying after I walked out," he said, followed by a brief silence. "You must be as screwed up inside as I am."

James stayed almost perfectly still, furrowing his brow while staring straight ahead at nothing, turning inside himself the way he often did. Blank.

Sebastian sensed his brother's apprehension.

"It's okay, ya know. It's okay to not be okay. I'm all screwed up inside, too."

James didn't respond at first. He wasn't as talkative as his brother.

"Did you ever talk to Mom about the way he treats us?" he finally said.

"I tried to talk to her about it once," said Sebastian. "She didn't wanna hear it. She took Dad's side, saying what a good provider he is and how he's really a good father and how we just don't appreciate him or respect him."

"I tried to talk her, too," James replied. "I was ten. Pretty much the same thing . . . how great Dad is and crap like that."

"I hate that!" Sebastian blurted. "I *hate* whenever someone comes up and tells me how great Dad is. 'Your father is such a great guy,'" he said in a sarcastic, nasally voice.

Both boys laughed, but then neither said anything for a few minutes, each glimpsing the other's eyes, acknowledging the magnitude of their conversation. Sebastian was recalling all the times someone told him what a great man their father is, like Mr. McCready at the picnic. James was remembering his conversation with Mr. King, the assistant principal, how he thought so much of their father.

"You know Mr. King at school?" James asked.

Sebastian nodded.

"He told me that he admires Dad . . . even said I should be more like him."

Sebastian shook his head in disbelief.

"What a dillhole," he said. "They're *all* dillholes."

"Our family's pretty screwed up, huh?" said James.

"You know, I started lifting weights to impress Dad," said Sebastian." I was sick and tired of being called a wussy or a wimp all the time. That's what drove me to work out so much. I pushed myself hard."

"Yeah, I remember you were really into it," said James. "You worked out at school, in the garage. You used to arm wrestle every guy at school."

"Yeah, I was into it for sure."

"Heck, I even remember how you used to drink a glass of raw eggs for breakfast like Rocky, and you'd ask Mom to cook liver for dinner to get more protein."

Day Five

"I just really, *really* wanted to be strong," replied Sebastian. "But for the record, I hated those raw eggs and liver. Thank God for powdered protein."

James laughed. He always thought it was disgusting when Sebastian swallowed a glass of raw eggs, the yellow yolks sliding down his throat like a slimy loogie.

"I remember when you set that world record," he said. "How much did you lift again?"

"Two hundred and five kilos."

"How much is that in pounds?" James asked.

"Four hundred and fifty-one pounds," Sebastian boasted.

"Damn, that's a lot! My gonads hurt just thinking about it. I remember when you came home and told Dad. He didn't even look up from the newspaper. He just said . . . "

". . . You think you're *better* than me?" Sebastian interrupted, imitating his father's stern tone.

"That's *exactly* the way he said it," James said, laughing so hard he snorted. "It's not funny, but it is in a way. I wasn't as strong as you or nothing, but I just started fighting back every time he'd call me a candy-ass or put me down. We had some pretty big blow outs. He almost killed me a couple times, but I got in some good punches myself, even gave him a bloody nose once. Now it seems like we fight all the time . . . Seems like I'm *always* fighting," said James, his voice trailing off. "I'm so tired, Sebastian . . . tired of everything."

Sebastian said nothing.

James cleared his throat before continuing.

"When I was lying there . . . buried in the snow . . . in the avalanche . . . I thought I was going to die, and I was scared at first, ya know, but there was this other part of me that wanted to die. I remember thinking it was the only way I could . . . escape. Escape *this* . . . escape *me*," he said, his eyes turning red and filling with tears.

Sebastian looked away from his brother's pain.

"Come on, let's play some more cards," he said, shuffling the deck and trying to sound cheerful. "How about something simple like Go Fish?"

Sunday, July 6, 1980

THE TENT WALLS WERE BUCKLED almost on top of them when Sebastian awoke in the morning. It was surprisingly dark inside the tent for midsummer.

"What the heck?" he said aloud, trying to push away the sagging orange ceiling only inches from his face. Any lower and they might have been smothered in their sleep.

The tent walls were covered with a thin, brittle crust of hoarfrost from their breathing throughout the night. As Sebastian's hands pressed against the ceiling, a sheet of frost fell onto his face.

"What the heck?" he said again, louder, brushing ice from his face.

He looked over at his brother.

"Hey! Wake up!" he said shaking James' sleeping lump. "Rise and shine."

"Wha . . . what is it?" James replied groggily, half asleep.

"Look."

"Whoa," replied James, looking at the nearly flattened tent ceiling above him.

"Must've snowed last night," said Sebastian. "Help me get the snow off the tent."

Still inside their sleeping bags, the boys managed to get on

121

their knees and used their shoulders to raise the ceiling, slapping the sides of the tent at the same time. As snow slid off the outside of the tent, they could see more daylight through the orange nylon. The mantle of rime on the inside broke off the ceiling and side walls, covering everything inside the tent like a delicate, crystalline dust.

"We better take a look outside," said Sebastian, lacing up his bunny boots. "Damn, it's cold this morning."

A heavy snowfall poured out of the leaden sky. The boys could barely see five feet in front of them when they scrambled out of the tent. The snow was almost waist-deep, and the sideways wind piled drifts against the cliff face. The temperature had fallen to maybe 20 degrees, not cold on a winter day, but unexpected in July. Of course, the boys were more than two miles into the atmosphere. The wind chill factor drove the apparent temperature down to 10 or 15 degrees below zero.

The tent looked as if it stood in a hole.

They worked carefully on the narrow ledge to clear snow from around the tent, and then crawled back inside to make breakfast—oatmeal again with powdered milk and a handful of raisins and nuts, washed down with cups of instant coffee. With the weight of the snow removed, the tent shook violently in the wind.

"What's the plan, Stan?" James asked, finishing the last sip of coffee in his stainless steel mug.

"I'm not sure," replied Sebastian. "I don't think we should risk it in this blizzard. We could hardly see the ground in front of us. We might walk right off a ledge. Imagine what it would be like trying to cross the glacier right now?"

James looked as if he were imagining the crevasses with their gaping mouths obscured in the flurry.

"That could be rough," he said.

"I think our best option is to hunker down here and wait out the storm . . . hope it blows itself out, or the wind shifts and pushes it elsewhere."

Day Six

James agreed.

For the rest of the day they lay inside their sleeping bags, trying to stay warm, getting up only to go outside and take care of nature's business as quickly as possible. The growling wind was so cold that their eyes would water and freeze shut when they blinked. Sebastian melted snow for hot tea or chicken or beef bouillon to warm their insides and keep them hydrated. Through gloved hands, Sebastian read *Hamlet* while James played his harmonica.

Sebastian recognized that his brother was playing "Me and Bobby McGee," one of his favorite songs with its message of freedom.

James stopped playing and knocked the harmonica against his open palm, draining the saliva before it froze solid.

"Why does she take a *harpoon* out of her bandana?" asked James.

"What?" asked Sebastian, looking up from his book.

"Janis . . . in her song . . . she says she took her *harpoon* out from her dirty, red bandana. I mean, what's . . . ?"

"It's another word for a harmonica, moron. Besides, Kris Kristofferson wrote the song, not Janis Joplin."

"Oh."

James chewed on the thought while Sebastian—hoping that was an end to the matter—returned peacefully to the slings and arrows of Hamlet's outrageous fortune, when James interrupted again.

"Why do they call it a harpoon?"

"How the hell should I know? Do I look like an encyclopedia?" Sebastian grumbled.

"No, but you look like the kind of nerd who reads encyclopedias. Harpoon . . . Har-POON. HAR-poon. That's stupid," James muttered.

Sebastian returned to reading. James played his harmonica again, but he stopped a few minutes later.

"Dad screwed us up royally, huh?" he said sadly. "I mean the way he treats us . . . the way he's *always* treated us."

Sebastian set his book aside. His expression turned thoughtful as he chose the right words.

"Yeah . . . but we aren't bad. You know that, right, despite all the mean crap he says about us. There was nothing we could have done to stop it. We were kids. Just kids."

"I know. I do. I get it," replied James. "But I don't think I can forget about it."

"I didn't say you have to forget about it. Who could? I just mean we need to . . . to *deal* with it."

It suddenly dawned on Sebastian why he it had been so important to bring *Hamlet* to read on this trip. Hamlet didn't ask for his life to be turned upside down the way it was. He was also victim of a terrible situation in which he had either to act to change it or roll over and accept it. Like Hamlet, Sebastian and James had been alone with their anguish, with no one to talk to and unsure of what to do.

"But I'm *really* messed up," said James, his voice aggravated. "I just don't care about anything. I hate everything and everyone."

Sebastian thought about James's tough-guy persona and his self-destructive behavior, like drinking all the time and smoking pot. He thought about his rotten attitude at school.

"You can't escape from your feelings," he said. "Trust me, I know. You have all these emotions bottled up . . . humiliation . . . helplessness . . . frustration, all locked up inside . . . but also rage. You're mad at the whole damn world."

"That's *exactly* how I feel!" James said.

"I'm mad, too, you know. I even hate God." Sebastian's anger grew suddenly hot.

James was taken aback by his brother's scornful words.

"Why didn't he give us a father who didn't screw up his kids and make them feel like crap all the time? Why couldn't I have had a father who loves me?" Sebastian continued, his eyes welling up.

"I don't know," James replied.

"What did I do to deserve this?" Sebastian cried. "I try to be good. I work hard at school. I clean my room. I try to be a good person . . . a good son. I do *everything everyone* asks of me. But it's never good enough for him," he sobbed, wiping his eyes.

James put a comforting hand on his brother's shoulder.

"I know you do," he said. "But I think that's part of your problem. You always want everyone to like you. You're always trying to impress everyone. I know it's because Dad never takes notice of anything you do, 'cause of the way he treats you, but you can't expect everyone to like you, Sebastian. It doesn't work that way. Stop trying to impress people. Just do things for yourself . . . because *you* want to . . . because it's what's right for *you*. Stop caring what other people think all the time and you'll be happier."

"Yeah. You're probably right," said Sebastian. "But what about you! You act like you've got something to prove, too. You think wearing a black leather jacket and carrying a switchblade makes you tough, like nothing can hurt you or your feelings. But all the crap you pull is only hurting yourself."

"What do you mean?" asked James, suddenly defensive.

"Getting into fights all the time at school. Getting bad grades. Smoking pot and drinking. It doesn't make what happened go away. You're at war with yourself. I can't blame you. Keep it up and you'll never graduate high school or go to college or get a decent job. You'll probably end up in jail. You'll be a loser, just like Dad says you are. You're letting him win."

"You don't think I think about that?" James snapped. "I think about that every single day. It's not just anger that I feel but . . . but . . . *rage*. I have so much hate inside me."

"No duh!" Sebastian replied. "I think that's part of the reason we fight each other so much—because we feel powerless to stop Dad or to fight back, so we strike out against each other instead. But you also fight the whole damned world. Remember last semester when you picked a fight with a gang at school? They kicked your ass."

James nodded, recalling the beating he took behind the gymnasium.

"It's like you have a death wish, or something."

"Like I haven't heard that before," James said, remembering what Mr. King had said.

"It's not funny. I mean it. Don't let the past destroy your future."

"That's really corny," said James. "You sound like a fortune cookie. Dad's right. You are a girl. I think I'm gonna puke."

They laughed.

James suddenly got a strange look on his face.

"Oh, damn!" he said, unzipping his sleeping bag and sitting upright.

"What's wrong?"

"I gotta take a leak."

The never-ending day slid by as slowly as a glacier. There's not much to do during a blizzard inside a tiny tent strapped to a ledge 12,000 feet above sea level. To make matters worse, the storm wasn't letting up as Sebastian had hoped. It raged on, the ferocious winds driving the temperature down to -20 and accelerating the ice crystals in spindrift to velocities fast enough to blast paint off a car. To stay warm, Sebastian and James huddled inside their sleeping bags wearing every bit of clothing they had brought along, regardless of how dirty and smelly. Several times the tent strings broke or the grommets ripped loose from the lashing nylon tent, and one of the boys had to go outside to repair the damage to their lifesaving shelter with bare hands.

Within minutes, exposed fingers were nearly frostbitten.

Around six in the evening, after repairing a line that had snapped, James crawled back inside the tent and shimmied into his sleeping bag.

Day Six

"God, it's cold out there!" he shouted above the howling tempest, rubbing his gloved hands together to warm them.

"What?"

"I said it's cold! I'm hungry!"

"What?"

"I said I'm HUNGRY!" James yelled above the sound of the shuddering tent walls. "What's for dinner?"

Sebastian rooted through his open pack, pulling out a package of dehydrated food.

"And the winner is . . . chili mac," he declared with a giant grin.

"No! No! For the love of God! Anything but that!" James pleaded. "What else is there?"

Sebastian reached in and fished out another package.

"How about beef stroganoff?" he shouted, reading the label.

"Anything's better than chili," replied James. "My nose couldn't survive it."

Monday, July 7, 1980

THE NIGHT PASSED MISERABLY for the boys trying to stay warm inside their sleeping bags. Almost hourly, the tent guylines broke, causing the slack wall to flutter so hard and snap so loudly that it was impossible to sleep. Sebastian and James took turns going outside to repair the damage.

"Get up. It's your turn," Sebastian groused.

"I did it last time," moaned James, turning over and snuggling deeper into his green mummy bag.

The scenario played out numerous times.

When the brothers finally did decide to get up and have some breakfast and coffee, it had stopped snowing, but the tempestuous winds hadn't let up a knot.

"I don't think we can climb down in this weather," said Sebastian. "A gust could blow us right off the mountain. Besides, even with our goggles on we might not be able to see through the spindrift blowing off the ridges. I say we wait it out a little longer . . . see what happens."

"I hate sitting in here. There's nothing to do," replied James, brooding. "And it's really starting to reek of funk."

"Knock-knock," said Sebastian.

"Seriously?"

"Come on. Knock-knock."

"Who's there?"

"Ugh."

James sighed.

"Ugh who?"

"You sure are ugly!" Sebastian sniggered.

"That doesn't even make sense. I gotta get outta this tent."

By noon, the wind had died down considerably, but the temperature still hovered around zero. Sebastian took stock of the food in his backpack.

"We can't stay up here much longer," he said. "There's only enough food for a couple days, and it's a long way to the truck."

Both knew the importance of food in mountaineering. As strenuous as it is—sometimes fourteen to sixteen hours of rigorous climbing a day—climbers need lots of energy. Also, it's hard to stay warm on an empty stomach. The body needs calories to convert into energy.

"Great! We'll starve and freeze to death up here," declared James. "So, what are we gonna do?"

"I think we give it a shot . . . get down the mountain while the getting's good."

"You mean right now?"

"Right now," said Sebastian, getting onto his knees and rolling up his sleeping bag. "Let's make like geese and get the flock outta here."

"That joke is so lame," said James, shaking his head in disbelief. "But anything beats sitting in here for another day."

Half an hour later, a hole in the snow where the tent had stood was the only evidence there had ever been a camp on the ledge.

Before setting out, the boys studied the route down the mountain. The knife-edged ridge line they had traversed several days earlier was buried in snow and drifts, making the descent ten times more difficult than their ascent. Blanketed as it was, with heavy overhangs, it would be nearly impossible to discern the topography underneath. One misstep could spell disaster. The 3,000-foot fall on either side would be deadly. Below the ridge, the boys could see the wide glacier, its crevasses concealed more than ever.

"Boy, this could be bad," said James, adjusting his goggles.

"Hey, look at the bright side," Sebastian replied happily.

"Yeah? What's that?"

"We still have the package of chili mac."

"Oh, joy," replied James, rolling his eyes.

They played it safe, long-roping their way down the ridge. James took point, leading the descent about a hundred feet ahead of Sebastian, dragging fifty feet of slack rope behind him. The blasting winds had sculpted the overhangs so that the crest of the thick-snowed ridge was precarious. Sometimes, chunks of packed snow the size of a car broke away beneath James's feet and hurtled down the 3,000-foot vertical cliff face.

Sebastian was careful to step in his brother's footprints, thinking that if James had made it safely, then he should as well.

The two tiny specks had worked their way down the ridge for an hour when, suddenly, Sebastian heard a scream. He looked up just in time to see James vanish off the north side of the mountain. The slack rope between them reeled rapidly forward. In an instant, Sebastian knew what had happened. The snow had given away, and James had plummeted off the cliff face. In a second, the rope would be pulled taut and yank Sebastian off the mountain as well. The brothers would perish together at the base of the cliff, more than 2,000 feet below. Straight away, Sebastian launched himself into thin air off the south side of the ridge, praying that the rope would hold. With a jolt his free fall was arrested, and he was slammed against the rock face. The impact hurt his right shoulder.

Snow and ice from above avalanched down on him.

Sebastian hung motionless at first, forcing his mind to stay conscious and taking stock of his situation. The fact that he wasn't falling meant that James was still connected to the other side, a counterweight. But he didn't know if his brother was still alive or dead. Sebastian shouted, but the wall of mountain between them blocked any communication.

Sebastian wasn't sure what to do. He couldn't just climb back up to the top. Once he stood on the crest, his brother's weight would pull him off the north side of the mountain. He certainly couldn't cut the rope. He slowly formed a plan and began climbing toward the top of the crest. When he was close, he hammered a piton into the rock face and connected himself to it with a carabineer and a short piece of rope; anchored that way, he couldn't be dragged off the other side.

Fortunately, when Sebastian scrambled onto the snow-thick ridge, he saw James just climbing over the north side less than a hundred feet below him.

He cupped his hand around his mouth and shouted to his brother. "You okay?"

James gave a thumbs-up with his gloved hand.

Sebastian responded with the hand signal that meant *hold up*. He disconnected himself from the anchored rope and worked his way down, careful to step in his brother's footprints. James's nose was streaming blood, running down his chin, bright red drops dripping on the pristine snow.

"I think I busted my nose," James announced when they were standing side by side.

Sebastian removed his pack and dug out what looked like a dark blue hand cloth.

"Here, use this to stop the bleeding," he said.

James took the wadded up cloth and pressed it against his bloody face.

"Holy smokes! That was scary! I thought we were dead," Sebastian declared with a smile and sigh of relief. "Don't ever do that again!"

"I think I crapped myself!" James muffled through the cloth.

Day Seven

"I can't believe we survived that." Sebastian laughed light-heartedly, looking over the precipice.

"That was pretty smart thinking . . . jumping off the other side like that," said James.

The brothers slapped a high-five.

"I saw my life flash before my eyes," said James. "I can't wait to get off this damn mountain."

"I'm sure glad there was some slack in the line," said Sebastian. "Otherwise, we'd both be dead by now."

After a couple minutes, James removed the blue cloth to see if his nose was still bleeding. A puzzled expression came over his face as he unwadded it.

"Wha . . . What the hell?" he exclaimed in horror. "Dude! This is your dirty underwear!"

"It's all I could find in a hurry," Sebastian said.

"Oh, man! I was nose deep in your nasty skid marks! Sick!"

"You'll live. Besides, it'll give me something to rag you about for the rest of your life."

"Oh, man . . ." said James, tossing the bloody underwear off the side of the cliff. "I can't *believe* you gave me that!"

"How's your nose?"

James gently pinched the bridge of his nose and wiggled it.

"It's not broken," he said. "What about you?"

Sebastian massaged his shoulder and shrugged a couple times.

"I hurt my shoulder. But it seems okay. Probably gonna have one hell of a bruise."

After a brief respite to calm their nerves, the brothers resumed their descent. This time Sebastian took point.

They made it safely to the edge of the glacier. Sebastian searched for an hour for the stone marker he had made to indicate the spot where they had crossed days before. But deep and drifted snow from the blizzard had buried everything, making it impossible to discern the stack of rocks from the white landscape.

"I think this is about the right spot," Sebastian stated reluctantly, after studying the surrounding geography to reckon their route across.

"I don't know," replied James with doubt in his voice. "I thought it was way back up there. It all looks the same to me."

"Well, we gotta cross somewhere. We can't stand around here forever," said Sebastian, climbing down to the surface of the glacier.

The boys long-roped their way slowly across the mile-wide ice field. The blanket of new snow made it difficult to see differences in the topography, but worse, it concealed crevasses. The brothers took turns leading the way. Whoever was at the rear carried Sebastian's ice ax, in case the leader fell into an icy abyss.

After an hour, the boys came upon a moulin canyon made from meltwater flowing on the surface of the glacier, carving its way down into the ice and blocking their progress. As far as they could see, the smooth-carved streambed snaked its way down the glacier for a long way in both directions.

"I think we have to cross it," said Sebastian.

"No way I'm crossing that!" replied James, remembering what had happened to the boy who fell into a moulin and would lie frozen beneath the glacier for a thousand years.

"I'll go first," said Sebastian, pulling out one of his ropes. "I'll rappel down this side, jump over the stream, and climb up the other side using the ax. Once I'm safe, I'll help you up."

James agreed. Digging the teeth of his crampons deep into the ice, he braced himself and payed out rope steadily as Sebastian rappelled down the canyon-like wall of ice.

When Sebastian was at the bottom of the ravine, he jumped across the shallow, four-foot stream, and began climbing the opposite wall, plunging his ax into the ice and using the forward-facing toe spikes of his crampons to climb up. The rope hung loosely from Sebastian's waist as James belayed from the other side, just in case he fell into the rushing stream of snowmelt with its smooth-polished bed. It was strenuous work, but Sebastian made it to the top of the other side of the canyon.

"Alright! Your turn!" he yelled across the icy chasm.

"Piece of cake!" James shouted back.

Before rappelling, James drove a long piton into the ice at an angle away from his descent. He hooked a carabineer to it and clipped in his end of the rope. That way, once he was safely down the ice wall and across the moulin stream, he could untie himself and Sebastian could pull the rope through, leaving the piton and carabineer embedded in the glacier forever, a monument to indicate where the brothers had crossed.

After James made his way down, jumping across the stream, Sebastian tossed down the rope and pulled him up.

An hour later, after avoiding several crevasses, the boys had made it across the glacier. They were exhausted.

"I'm starved. We haven't had anything to eat since breakfast," James griped.

"Me too. Let's set up camp and have something hot to eat," replied Sebastian. "I need to get this pack off my back. My shoulder's killing me."

After setting up camp, Sebastian took off his sweatshirt to examine his shoulder.

"Whoa! That's a doozy!" exclaimed James. "Looks like you got hit by a freight train."

"How bad is it?" asked Sebastian, who could only see the top of his shoulder.

"Dude, your entire shoulder and upper back is black and blue. Does it hurt?"

"Not really. Just where the shoulder straps were."

James jabbed a finger into the bruise.

"Ouch!"

"I guess it does," said James.

Sebastian put his shirt back on and rummaged through his pack looking for something to cook for dinner. He found only the package of dehydrated chili and macaroni. Almost frantically, he started pulling out everything from his pack.

"They've gotta be in here," he said to himself.

"What's wrong?" asked James, unrolling his sleeping bag atop his blue foam sleeping bad.

"I swear I had four more packages of food in here," replied Sebastian. "Enough for two days."

James looked concerned.

"Did you check the side pockets?"

"Of course!" Sebastian barked.

"Hey, don't get mad at me," said James. "How could you not bring enough food?"

"I bought enough packages so that we could have two hot meals twice a day. I know I did."

"Well, where are they?"

"I dunno. I remember seeing them in a white plastic bag before we packed camp . . ."

Sebastian suddenly remembered what he had done with them.

"Oh, shit!" he cried out. "I set the bag outside when we were taking everything out of the tent. I must not have noticed it in the snow when we left."

"Great! I'm not crossing that glacier again and climbing back up that ridge for nothing," declared James. "No way! How much food is there?"

"Besides the chili and mac, just a little bit of oatmeal and some trail mix," replied Sebastian, holding up a partial sandwich baggie of mixed nuts, M&Ms, and dried fruit.

"Well . . . Crap! We're a hell of a long way from the nearest grocery store! I can't *believe* you lost our food!" James shouted, inches from his brother's face.

"Get off my back!" Sebastian shouted, pushing James away.

James calmed down. He knew he wasn't strong enough to take Sebastian.

"What are we gonna do?" he said.

138

Day Seven

Sebastian looked into the empty backpack again, shaking his head in disbelief.

"I guess we eat the friggin' chili tonight and stretch out the oatmeal for as long as we can."

"Great! Chili in a tent!" said James. "Just shoot me now."

That night, snug in his sleeping bag, Sebastian had a series of nightmares. In the first one, an army of topless teenage girl zombies were chasing him, but Bruce Lee magically appeared and helped him escape using Kung Fu. In another, James bashed his brains out with a rock and was roasting one of his legs over the small cook stove, seasoning it with salt and pepper. Sebastian woke up, startled. The sound awoke James, who opened his eyes only for an instant, grunted, coughed, and then rolled over, farted, and fell back into his sonorous sleep.

Sebastian lay with one eye open for a long time.

Tuesday, July 8, 1980

THE LAST DAY ON THE MOUNTAIN. That's what Sebastian thought while rubbing sleep from his crusted eyes when he awoke in the morning. As his hands touched his face, he felt his course beard and moustache—the result of eight or nine days without shaving. He looked at his wristwatch.

5:43 AM.

Deciding to let his brother sleep a little longer, Sebastian quietly dug out his book and read the last pages. When he was finished, he set the book down, pulled his hands inside his sleeping bag to warm them, and stared at the tent ceiling. Tears formed in the corners of his eyes. Sebastian didn't want the story of his life and struggle to end the way Hamlet's did, with his own death, surrounded by destruction, as if he took the whole damn world down with him. He wanted a better resolution, one he could live with, even if uneasily at times.

But almost as much as Sebastian worried about himself, looking over at his sleeping brother, he worried that James might not fare as well . . . that the end of *his* story might be more like Hamlet's end—volatile and self-destructive. Such was his brother's querulous nature. At only seventeen, Sebastian already understood that too many people waste their lives wishing to relive bygone moments when one event or one bad decision led them down a miserable path.

He knew because he was one of them.

When he thought it was time to get moving, Sebastian unzipped the tent door and scooped snow in the pot to melt for water. As always, the small stove warmed the tent. James awoke to the smell of coffee.

"I'll take a cup of that," he said groggily, sitting up in his sleeping bag and running a hand through his tussled hair. "What's for breakfast?"

"Nada. We have to ration the oatmeal," replied Sebastian. "We'll have it for lunch or linner."

"What the hell is linner?"

"In between lunch and dinner . . . linner. You know . . . like brunch."

"So, this lousy cup of coffee is all we get?" asked James.

"Unless you got some steak and eggs in your backpack, it is."

James pulled his pack closer and reached deep into a side pocket, pulling out a chocolate candy bar.

"I've been saving this," he said. "We can split it. At least it has some calories."

James opened the brown wrapper, broke the scored bar in two, and handed half to Sebastian.

"Thanks."

After eating their meager breakfast, the boys broke camp and continued their descent. Gravity pulled them downhill. Several hours later, after making good time, they stopped for lunch. Still above the tree line, surrounded by snow and rock, Sebastian used the small cook stove to heat water for the oatmeal. The flame flickered and died just as the water came to a boil. They were out of food, out of sugar and powdered creamer for their coffee and oatmeal, out of clean clothes, and now they were even out of fuel to heat water. Sebastian scooped equal portions into two bowls, handing one to James.

Day Eight

"Here. That'll stick to your ribs," he said.

They ate their bland meal in silence.

"So what are you gonna do when we get home?" asked James, using his spoon to scrape out every last bit of oatmeal.

"What do ya mean?"

"I mean about . . . us . . . life . . . Dad."

Sebastian thought about his response before answering.

"I'm not sure, but I know one thing: I'm not gonna give the jerk the satisfaction of hurting me anymore. He can do his worst, but I'm not gonna let it get to me."

James nodded. "Yeah . . . Me, too."

Sebastian knew it would be more difficult for James to hold his tongue and tolerate their father's abuse. It was just his nature.

"I've been thinking about moving out," Sebastian said matter-of-factly.

"But you're barely seventeen," replied James.

"I know. But I have a part-time job, saved up some money. I could rent a cheap place or split the rent with someone."

"What about school?" James asked.

"I'd finish. I like school. I wanna go to college . . . become a teacher or a writer."

"So, you're just gonna leave me alone with Dad?"

"I don't know what else to do."

"Maybe we could talk to someone," said James. "A teacher like Mr. Betters."

"Everyone thinks Dad is so great," replied Sebastian. No one's going to help us."

"But there's two of us," said James. "If we stick together we could . . ."

Sebastian shook his head.

"Maybe I could live with you? Nah. That wouldn't work. I know! We could *off* Dad instead. Push him off a cliff or boat or something . . . kick out the floor jack when he's under the car changing the oil so it looks like an accident. Nah . . . That

145

wouldn't be right. Would it?" asked James, with a playful yet deadly serious tone.

Sebastian didn't reply.

"Did you hear what I said? Would it be wrong to get rid of Dad? You know . . . a dirt nap?"

"Hmm," replied Sebastian, looking thoughtful. "I got nothing."

Late in the afternoon, with the sun perched on the craggy teeth of the mountain, the brothers made it back to the small alpine lake where they had camped on the way up, where they'd had the encounter with the grizzly bear in their tent. They stumbled upon a dead moose covered in dirt amid a thicket of alder bushes.

The brothers knew what it was immediately.

"Bear kill," they both said, looking at the partially eaten carcass.

Sebastian and James knew that a bear will eat however much it takes to fill its belly, cover the rest of the kill to stay cool and to keep away flies—a kind of natural bear pantry—and then come back later for more. Often, the bear lies nearby sleeping off its meal.

"Let's get the hell out of here," James whispered, backing away from the kill.

Sebastian started to follow his brother, but then stopped. He looked around.

"What are you doing? C'mon!" whispered James.

"Dinner," said Sebastian, unsheathing his folding hunting knife on his belt.

"Are you crazy? We gotta get outta here! That bear could be anywhere," James said, his eyes darting anxiously across the alpine landscape.

Sebastian knelt beside the moose, brushed away dirt and moss, and cut a roast-sized hunk of meat from the hindquarter. The meat was firm and cool to the touch, a sign that it hadn't spoiled. Sebastian smelled it. It smelled fresh.

Day Eight

"Okay. Let's scram," he said, holding up the chunk of red meat.

Almost at a jog, the boys distanced themselves from the moose kill. All the while they blew their whistles hanging from their jacket zippers and sang a medley of songs from the movie *Grease* at the top of their lungs. They understood that when in bear country, it's best to avoid close encounters. Let the bear know *what* and *where* you are. That's the best policy.

Well below the tree line, along the gravel bank of a clear brook, the brothers finally stopped, set up camp, built a blazing campfire, and roasted the moose meat on sticks held over the flames. That night, they slept restlessly, waking to every little sound, fearful that a bear was following their scent, planning its revenge.

Wednesday, July 9, 1980

JAMES PUNCHED SEBASTIAN SEVERAL TIMES through his sleeping bag.

"Wake Up . . . Bear," he whispered anxiously.

"What?"

"Sshh . . . I think there's a bear outside," he said, putting his index finger to his lips and then pointing toward the front of the tent.

The boys sat motionless, straining to hear even the smallest sound. Sebastian reached for his folding Buck knife and opened it smoothly until it clicked.

"What are ya gonna do with that?" James remarked quietly.

"Defend myself. What do ya think?"

"You gonna fight a bear with a knife? Good luck with that," replied James.

"What do you think I should do," asked Sebastian, still whispering.

"Bend over and kiss your booty goodbye."

A rustling noise outside the tent, clearly audible to both boys, riveted their attention.

"Did you hear that?" asked James, almost in a panic.

Sebastian nodded and brandished his knife, ready to defend himself when the bear ripped open the tent.

Terrified, James fumbled for his pants with his black leather knife sheath on the belt.

"Be quiet," said Sebastian. "It'll hear you."

For the longest couple of minutes in history, the boys listened to the rustling and scratching sound outside, which was very close to the tent now. They could hear their own hearts beating.

"Maybe it'll go away," said James, opening his hunting knife with trembling hands.

Then they heard a crunching sound.

"What the hell is it doing?" asked Sebastian.

"I don't know. We didn't leave anything outside to eat. Maybe it can smell that we roasted the moose meat over the fire."

Sebastian slowly unzipped the tent door, trying to make as little noise as possible. James got up onto his knees, his knife-wielding hand at the ready. Sebastian pulled back the orange nylon door so they could see what the bear was doing. About ten feet away, sitting on a fallen log, a squirrel was eating seeds from a pinecone.

The brothers burst into laughter. The terrified squirrel dropped its meal, scurried up a tree, and chattered at them angrily from the safety of a low branch.

"Holy cow! I thought that was a bear for sure," said James, closing his knife.

Sebastian put away his knife as well.

While breaking camp, the boys joked about the experience.

"Remember the killer rabbit in *Monty Python and the Holy Grail*?" asked Sebastian.

James laughed. It was one of his favorite movies.

"You know what a bear calls two boys in sleeping bags?" he asked.

Sebastian shrugged.

"Kids in a blanket . . . You get it? Like pigs in a blanket."

"Hardy-har-har," replied Sebastian. "What a knucklehead."

A little while later, the brothers said farewell to their campsite.

The Reckoning

"Goodbye killer squirrel!" James proclaimed loudly to the forest.

Without breakfast, they followed the creek down the mountain through trees and thick, almost impassable brush to the floodplain below. By then it was almost noon. At the confluence where the little creek merged with another clear creek, they saw that the water was almost choked with salmon, hundreds of them in a stream no wider than eight feet across and a foot deep.

"Lunch!" declared Sebastian with a broad grin.

After they removed their packs and their hiking boots and socks, and rolled up their jeans, James stepped into the icy water about fifty yards below where Sebastian stood—the school of unsuspecting salmon between them.

"Damn, it's cold!" said James.

On signal, the brothers walked noisily toward one another, kicking and splashing and waving their arms madly. The frightened fish swarmed in every direction. Several shot right out of the creek and onto the gravel banks. James chased after one while Sebastian chased after another, but Sebastian lost his when it managed to flip itself back into the creek. But James caught his. They built a campfire, gutted the fish, and roasted it on a willow stick over the fire.

"Delicious," said James, savoring a bite of the reddish-orange meat.

"I concur," Sebastian said, using a fake British accent. "Let's order up a bottle of wine. Shall we have red or white with salmon?"

James laughed.

"White, I think," he said.

After lunch, the brothers followed the creek to its confluence with the wide river they had crossed the afternoon they had arrived. But it no longer resembled the river they had easily forged, wading knee deep from sand bar to sand bar through gurgling riffles. The snowy blizzard high up on the mountain had produced rain storms and flashfloods below, and the warm summer sun had melted ice on the glacier. The river was swollen with water, threatening to flood its steep banks.

Sebastian and James stood looking at the river, dumbfounded. They hadn't expected this. It hadn't even occurred to them. What had been merely an inconvenience eight days earlier was now downright dangerous. Trees raced by, swept downstream after root-clinging banks had been undercut by the swift, gouging current. Judging from the water level, Sebastian figured the river was ten feet deep—almost a million gallons of water racing by every minute.

Sebastian sat down on a boulder. James sat down beside him, both facing the torrent.

"How are we going to get across *that*?" asked James. "I sure the hell ain't swimmin' across!"

"I have no idea," replied Sebastian.

For half an hour the brothers explored their options. Since they hadn't told anyone where they were going, they couldn't expect help to arrive. Few people traveled the rugged road to where they could see Sebastian's small gray truck parked on the other side. They were out of food. They were out of coffee and tea. They were out of clean clothes. They couldn't wait out the flood . . . it could take weeks for the water to go back down so they could safely wade across. And it might not go down at all with the July sun melting glaciers in the high country.

Sebastian looked back at the mountain, which seemed less inhospitable from such a distance. Then he looked at his truck, parked only a few hundred yards away.

"So close and yet so far," he said, nodding his head.

He opened his pack, dug out his blue parka, and fished out the photographs of him and James at the summit from an inside pocket.

The brothers sat looking at the pictures, talking about their experience almost nostalgically, the way Sebastian had planned they would for the rest of their lives.

Finally, James had an idea.

"I know . . . we can make a raft, like Huckleberry Finn."

Sebastian stood up.

"Now that's a good idea!" he said, excitedly stuffing his parka back into his pack and shoving the photographs inside his jacket pocket.

They decided their best plan was to go far up river to build their raft. They knew they couldn't fight the current and paddle straight across. By starting upriver, they could work their way to the other side little by little, ending up near where the truck was parked.

Congratulating themselves on their quick thinking, Sebastian and James followed the shoreline for half a mile or longer. They found a perfect place to build and launch their raft. It took only an hour to scrounge enough logs—each about five or six inches across—and drag them to the water's edge, where they built an irregular-shaped platform secured with climbing rope. Although the raft was about five feet wide, without a saw, the length was composed of a variety of logs: eight-footers, some ten-footers, and a couple that were even close to twelve or thirteen feet long. The resulting craft was ungainly and shabby, but it would float. Their short snow shovels would have to serve as paddles.

All in all, their plan seemed sound.

Using stout poles as levers, the boys managed to heave the raft into the water. Sebastian held the short tie-off rope.

"Jump on," he said. "Let's see how she floats with a load."

James stepped onto the unsteady raft, which appeared to support his weight. He got down on his knees in the middle.

Sebastian handed him the shovel-paddles.

"Here goes nothing," he said, as he jumped onto the middle of the raft behind his brother and got down onto his knees as well.

His added weight pressed the logs deeper into the river so that the entire raft was submerged under an inch of water. But it stayed afloat. At the same time, the current snatched the raft and sent it careening downriver, spinning slowly as it went.

"Let's straighten her out," said Sebastian, using his makeshift paddle to turn the bow downstream.

The current carried the raft faster than they had thought. The half-mile starting point seemed insufficient.

"Paddle on the right side!" shouted Sebastian.

Then a moment later, "Paddle on the left side! Harder!"

The raft made slow headway against the powerful current. In the middle of the river, the raft began to come apart.

"We're not going to make it!" James yelled as the gap between the logs became wider, and one of the shorter logs worked itself loose of its lashing.

"Faster! Paddle faster!" Sebastian shouted, digging the flat of his shovel deep into the water.

Half the length of a football field from shore, the raft came apart, spilling the boys into the muddy river. The dirty clothes, insulated winter coat, and sleeping bag inside their backpacks instantly became waterlogged, dragging them beneath the surface. The current turned them every which way. In darkness, with their lungs bursting for air, Sebastian and James clawed for the surface, struggling to remove their packs.

Finally, they emerged into the sunlight and gasped for air, choking and coughing. Sebastian swam to his brother about twenty feet away.

"We need . . . to get . . . to shore . . . as fast . . . as we can," he said, as waves splashed over his face.

Both knew the danger they were in. The water was so cold that their muscles would lock up in a matter of minutes and they would drown. Sebastian looked at the shore. They had already passed the spot where the truck was parked.

"Swim for it. Stay close." he said, his teeth already chattering.

But when they were close to shore, Sebastian could no longer raise his arms. In cold water, his lack of body fat was a detriment, reducing his buoyancy and his body's ability to stay warm.

"I . . . I can't . . . make . . . it," he said, barely able to speak, his head going under.

James wrapped his right arm around his brother's neck and, using his left arm—his strong arm—he dog-paddled toward shore, the current sweeping them downriver at a runner's pace. James swam with every bit of strength he had with his brother's head tucked in the crook of his arm. Sebastian's face was turned skyward, his eyes open, marveling at the quietude of the blue sky and drifting clouds. A curious raven flying overhead dipped to investigate. Finally, the brothers made it to the far bank. They slogged out of the river, bent double, barely able to stand, each with an arm around the other for support. Sebastian sat down to catch his breath, a puddle forming beneath him, the sun warming his trembling body. They had lost their packs with all their gear, but they were still alive.

"Thanks," said Sebastian. "We're two-and-two."

James understood how hard it was for Sebastian to accept help from anyone.

"You'd have done the same for me," he said.

Sebastian stood up, wiping dirt from the seat of his wet pants.

"Let's go home," he said, sounding exhausted.

In their squishing boots, the brothers trudged along the bank to the waiting truck, where Sebastian found the hidden keys where he had left them. He took off his sopping jacket, feeling something inside a pocket. He reached in and pulled out the few pictures he had taken at the summit. They were the only proof of their endeavor. The Polaroid camera, along with all the rest of the photographs, was inside his backpack at the bottom of the river.

They climbed into the truck and closed the squeaky doors. Sebastian started the engine and slid the heater lever to high, placing the photographs on the dashboard to dry out beside the snapshot of the mountain he had taken the day they arrived.

The long drive home was quiet. Within minutes, James fell asleep with his head against the window, lost in the bliss of deep sleep. Stupefied with weariness, Sebastian found it almost impossible to stay awake. Several times he dozed off momentarily, awakened brusquely by the loud rumbling of the tires driving over the drunk-bumps embedded along the edge of the road. At such times, he swerved sharply back into his lane.

"Stay awake," he'd say, slapping himself in the face. "Just a little further."

All the way home, Sebastian imagined the conversation they'd have with their father as they told him about their adventure and showed him the pictures.

Things are going to be different from now on, he thought, trying to keep his eyes open.

Sebastian and James could see their father's head through the living room window when they pulled into the driveway. He looked out when he heard the truck doors close. Dog-tired, the brothers dragged themselves up the carpeted stairs, each clutching a photograph of himself standing on the summit. Their father was sitting in his recliner reading the newspaper. *The Jeffersons* was on television. He didn't even look up when they came into the living room and stood before him.

Sebastian cleared his throat to announce they were home.

"How was Girl Scout Camp? You candy-asses learn how to knit and sew?" he chuckled, without looking up from the paper and without commenting that they were home a day early.

"It was okay," Sebastian replied. "We wanted to show you some . . ."

"I want you sissies to mow the lawn tomorrow and sweep out the garage," the father interrupted, without looking at his sons.

Both boys stared at him incredulously. There they stood, exhausted, hungry, and disheveled, bruised and battered, their faces raw from wind and sunburn, their noses and their lips chapped and peeling. Neither had combed his hair in over a week. Sebastian was sporting a scruffy full-faced beard.

"Sure, Dad," replied Sebastian, holding out his photograph, "but we wanted to . . ."

"Did you hear what I said?" the father barked. "And there's a pile of firewood out back by the gate. Stack it up and do it right or I'll make you do it again like last time."

Now both boys were trembling with anger. Twice they had braved the icy river. Twice they had traversed the perilous glacier. They had survived a blizzard, an avalanche, frostbite, hypothermia, drowning, a bear encounter, and even a death-defying free fall into thin air. Through hard work and sheer willpower, they had conquered the mountain, risking their lives over and over again. And now their father wasn't even giving them the chance to tell him about it or show him the pictures.

"And go take showers! I can smell you two losers from here."

James clenched his fist and stepped toward his father sitting behind the obscuring newspaper, but Sebastian pulled him back. James yanked his arm free and glared at his brother. Sebastian shook his head slowly and smiled. James relaxed, smiled back, and nodded in sudden understanding. They had conquered the mountain, but their father and the world they had returned to was much the same. Day by day, they would have the same challenges they had faced before. In the years to come, people would ask them why they had climbed the mountain, and the truth was they had done it for reasons they did not fully understand themselves. But this much they knew. Somewhere up there among the snow and ice and clouds *something* had happened to them. Somehow *they* had changed, even if the world hadn't changed with them.

With pictures in hand, Sebastian and James turned and walked down the hall toward their bedrooms. From behind them they could hear the rustle of newspaper as their father turned the page and shook the obedient paper flat.

"Lazy punks will never be half the man I am," he muttered, loud enough for them to hear.

From down the hall came laughter followed by the sound of closing doors.

Looking up from his newspaper, their father wondered what the hell the boys were laughing about now.

For almost a million years the mountain had resisted the forces endeavoring to destroy it: slow-moving glaciers gouging and scarring its bedrock, frost crumbling its crags and cliffs into dust, winter-lashing blizzards raging against its summit, and flash floods scouring the steep valleys and dales, washing its foundation to the sea. But no matter how harshly the world assailed it, the indomitable mountain persevered, resolute, able to withstand every abuse hurled against it.

Some sons are like a mountain.

Questions for Discussion

1. Describe the relationship between James and Sebastian at the beginning of the novel. How does their relationship change throughout the story?

2. How are Sebastian and James different from each other? Is James really as tough as he pretends to be? In what ways are you different from your brothers or sisters?

3. Mr. Savage always belittles Sebastian's blinking, mumbling, and stuttering, calling him an imbecile. Why do you think Sebastian only does these things whenever he's around his father?

4. Describe the relationship between the brothers and their father. In what ways is it abusive? Describe their relationship with their mother. Why doesn't she help her sons more?

5. Discuss the brothers' decision to climb the mountain. Does it seem incredulous? Would you agree that most children desire attention and love from their parents? What have you done to gain positive attention from your parents? How do you feel when they praise you? How do feel when they ignore or demean you?

6. Discuss the irony of how other people in town view Mr. Savage as a pillar of the community—a man's man—and the way he treats Sebastian and James.

7. At the end of their harrowing adventure, having risked their lives many times to prove themselves to their father, the boys didn't even get a chance to tell him what they had accomplished or to show him the proving photographs. Do you think it would have made a difference in their relationship if they had? Why did the brothers laugh at the end?

8. Some readers may question why the father is portrayed so flatly. Would making his character more complex have served a purpose? Can there be anything in his past—in any abuser's past—that excuses or pardons the abuse of others?

9. How does the book's title reflect the problems of the novel?

The Author

As a teenager, John Smelcer learned to mountain climb at the U.S. Army's Black Rapids Mountaineering School and at Outward Bound wilderness and climbing schools. He and his brother, James, climbed many of Alaska's peaks.

John is the author of over forty books. His first novel, *The Trap*, hailed as "a small masterpiece," was an American Library Association BBYA Top Ten Pick, a VOYA Top Shelf Selection, and a New York Public Library Notable Book. Listed among the greatest children's adventure stories of all time, *The Great Death* was short-listed for the 2011-2012 William Allen White Awards, one of the oldest awards in America for children's literature. *Edge of Nowhere* was named one of the "Best Teen Novels of 2010" in the United Kingdom. The US edition (Leapfrog Press, 2014) was highlighted by *School Library Journal's* Spotlight on Diverse Books. *Lone Wolves* (Leapfrog Press, 2013) has been hailed as one of the greatest adventure books for young readers and was a winner of the American Library Association's Amelia Bloomer Award for feminist literature. His collection of short stories, *Alaskan*, received a gold medal in the 2011 international *e*Lit Book Awards. Part of this novel was written in Talkeetna, the climbing capitol of Alaska.

Learn more at www.johnsmelcer.com.

Lone Wolves

John Smelcer

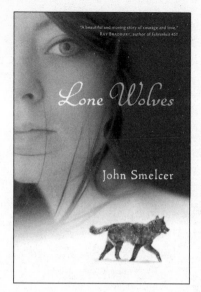

Deneena Yazzie isn't like other 16-year-old girls in her village. Her love of the woods and trail come from her grandfather, who teaches her the all-but-vanished Native Alaskan language and customs. While her peers lose hope, trapped between the old and the modern cultures, Denny and her mysterious lead dog, a blue-eyed wolf, train for the Great Race—a thousand-mile test of courage and endurance through the vast Alaskan wilderness. Denny learns the value of intergenerational friendships, of maintaining connections to her heritage, and of being true to herself, and in her strength she gives her village a new pride and hope.

"A beautiful and moving story of courage and love."
—Ray Bradbury

"With this inspiring young adult novel, Smelcer promises to further solidify his status as 'Alaska's modern-day Jack London.'"
—*Mushing* magazine, Suzanne Steinert

"Powerful, eloquent, and fascinating, showcasing a vanishing way of life in rich detail."
—*Kirkus*

"An engaging tale of survival, love, and courage."
—*School Library Journal*

Amelia Bloomer List of recommended feminist literature
(American Library Association)

Edge of Nowhere

John Smelcer

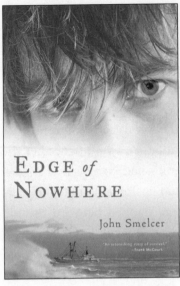

Sixteen-year-old Seth and his dog fall off his father's commercial fishing boat in Prince William Sound. They struggle to survive off land and sea as they work their way home from island to island in a three-month journey. The isolation allows Seth to understand his father's love, accept his Native Alaskan heritage, and accept his grief over his mother's death.

"Smelcer's prose is lyrical, straightforward, and brilliant . . . authentic Native Alaskan storytelling at its best."
—*School Library Journal*, starred review

"A spare tale of courage, love and terrible obstacles . . . may have special appeal to teens who like to wonder how they would do if they had to survive in the wild."
—*Wall Street Journal*

"Brief, thoughtful, and often lyrical, this is a quick pick for young teens who have the good sense not to confuse a short book with a shallow book."
—*Bulletin of the Center for Children's Books*

"More psychological depth than Robinson Crusoe."
—Frank McCourt

Chosen for the 2014 Battle of the Books by the Alaska Association of School Libraries

An American Booksellers Association ABC Best Books for Children title

Stealing Indians

a novel by

John Smelcer

Available Spring 2016

Excerpt from Chapter 1

Simon Lone Fight was running across an arid desert, dodging rattlesnakes and scorpions, jumping over tumbleweeds spinning across the red earth.

Simon was always running.

He ran to and from everything—from the grocery store to the service station where his uncle worked, from his ramshackle home to the community hall where everyone played bingo on Fridays and Saturday nights, from the future and toward the past. He ran all day across his reservation, which was so destitute that even the few small streams winding across the arid landscape were almost always empty-pocketed and bone-dry.

Simon ran across the hot, red desert, through its echoing canyons and arroyos, over buttes and mesas, jumping over boulders and tumbleweeds, startling jackrabbits and lizards, his long black hair shining in the sun.

No one on his reservation could keep up with him.

Even his shadow had to stop to rest, bent double under a high sun, winded, gray shadow-sweat dripping on the thirsty earth. No one had ever seen anything like him. He'd run up and down the highway, waving at cars and smiling the whole time. His mother used to joke that Simon went straight from crawling to running—just grabbed his milk bottle one day and took off running out the front door, his little, chubby baby legs carrying him all the way to the edge of the reservation before his father caught up with him in a pickup truck.

And he'd been running ever since.

Simon's parents died on his thirteenth birthday. Both of them, father and mother in a car crash going around Dead Man's Bend coming home from a funeral. When a drunk driver swerves toward you on a narrow turn with a 240-foot drop, there's no place to go, no place to run or hide, no safe space in all the world.

After his parents' funeral, Simon returned to his mobile home resting on cement blocks, changed out of his secondhand black suit and tie, which he had borrowed from his cousin who was several inches taller and more than a dozen pounds heavier, drank a glass of cold water in one long, breathless series of gulps, ate a bologna-and-cheese sandwich with pickles and sliced green tomatoes, and went out for a run.

He was gone for three days.

No one knew what had happened to Simon. The whole reservation heard about his disappearance. Men and women, boys and girls from all over went out looking for him. Twenty-seven pickups—all with mismatched tires and expired license plates—left the parking lot at Fat Mabel's Bar & Grill, each driver assigned a specific area to search. The congregation of the First Baptist Church of Indian Conversion cooked up a giant batch of fry bread to feed all the searchers. The police put out an all-points bulletin. Fliers were printed and circulated all over the reservation, stapled to utility poles, to storefronts, and duct-taped to abandoned trucks and empty fuel barrels rusting in fields. Someone even stapled signs at all five holes of Big Red Chief's Mini-Golf.

Even Simon's dog, Tonto, went out looking for him. They named the dog that because he followed the boy everywhere, like a faithful side-kick who couldn't speak a word of English.

Luckily, his second cousin on his father's side, Norman Fury, found him running along a backcountry road five towns over. He saw Simon at first from a distance, bouncing slightly with each jogging stride, saw him through heat waves writhing up from the melting, black asphalt, like an apparition only partly of this world.

The boy almost made it to the state line.

During the next year, Simon was passed from relative to relative, from one cramped house of poverty to another. No one even knew that his fourteenth birthday had come and gone. In all of his many moves he never once had a room of his own. Each time he moved, Tonto went with him. They were inseparable.

One day, Tonto, looking down the one lane dirt road, began to bark at a growing black dot on the burning horizon, a cloud of dust building behind it. Simon didn't know why he felt suddenly afraid of the black dot. He crept behind a corner of the house and watched as the approaching dot turned into a car. When it turned down their driveway, Simon and his dog scooted off, staying low and hiding behind the leaning outhouse—both trying not to breathe as they watched. From his crouching position, the boy saw two white men in dark suits with dark briefcases step out of the black, high-roofed automobile. His grandparents came out from their house to speak to the men. Simon couldn't hear a word they said, but it was clear that his grandfather was arguing with the men. After a while, his grandfather sat down on a small stool and dropped his head low, while his grandmother went inside the house, calling for Simon.

When she came out alone, the men went inside to search the house. By the time they started checking the yard and the outhouse, Simon was already a mile back in the canyons, running faster than he had ever run before, the panic swirling inside him, pushing him along like a hard wind.

The men came for him three more times that month, but Simon was always gone before they even turned off the heavy engine inside the chest of the big, black car.

One day at the end of summer, his grandparents told him they were going into town to sell hay. They asked Simon to come along, promising him ice cream if he helped unload the heavy bales. The cramped cab of the old truck allowed for only two, so Simon and Tonto jumped into the back and sat atop of the small cluster of bales. They loved riding in the open bed, the cooling rush of wind pouring over them as the truck sped down the road, jack rabbits jumping from the gravel shoulders.

Dark clouds were building on the horizon. A storm was approaching. Simon was worried that it would rain before they returned home.

But before they arrived in town, the truck turned on a road leading to a small train station at the edge of town, more whistle stop than station. Simon recognized the place. It was where ranchers sold their livestock for immediate loading on freight trains. His grandfather shut off the engine, climbed out from the cab, and closed the creaking door. His grandmother waited inside.

"Come on down from there, boy," he said, lowering the tailgate.

Simon and Tonto jumped down from the bed, kicking up dust as they landed.

"You gonna load these bales on the train, Grandpa?" Simon asked, confused because he had never known the old man to sell hay to anyone but locals. Besides, the dozen-or-so bales on the truck hardly made up a load worth shipping on a train.

His grandfather didn't answer but looked at his pocket watch instead.

"Five minutes," he said, as he slid the watch back into his pocket.

While they waited, Simon tossed sticks for Tonto to fetch. They were out in the nearby fields playing when the train whistled its arrival. Simon ran back, ready to help his grandfather. The locomotive engine was so loud that the boy didn't hear the high-roofed black car pulling up next to the old truck. Two men slid out like snakes and grabbed the boy from behind.

Simon struggled to break away, screaming. His dog barked and bit the leg of one of the men. His grandmother covered her eyes with her hands and wept inside the cab, the sun scorched the parched landscape, a lizard darted beneath a rock, and his grandfather stood by sullenly watching the whole thing, squeezing and squeezing his empty hands inside his empty pockets.

"You got to go with these men," he said, his voice filled with sadness.

"But I want to stay with you!" Simon cried, still trying to free himself.

The old man swallowed his love for his grandson, swallowed his love of his own dead son, and swallowed a thousand years of pride.

"You must go to school," he said. "It's the law."

The sound of those words made Simon hate the school already, whatever it was, wherever it was.

On an imitation leather seat aboard the train's passenger car, the young Indian boy who loved to run, who could outrun everything but this moment, looked out the window as the train started to move. The powerful engine picked up speed, and Simon watched as the only world he had ever known began to slide away: the mesas, the dull-pink earth beneath the vaulted sky, the arroyos and canyons, the thirsty fields, the hogans, and the government housing that all looked the same.

Simon watched his faithful dog running beside the train, barking at it as if he might turn the great machine around, just as he sometimes did wayward sheep. Simon watched him struggling to keep pace, until he could run no longer and slowed to a trot and then stopped altogether and sat in the middle of the tracks and howled.

For many rattling miles, Simon Lone Fight stared out the smudged glass, quietly crying, his heart bursting, his small brown hands pressed sadly against the latched window, closed tight as a fist.

About the Type

This book was set in Adobe Caslon, a typeface originally released by William Caslon in 1722. His types became popular throughout Europe and the American colonies, and printer Benjamin Franklin used hardly any other typeface. The first printings of the American Declaration of Independence and the Constitution were set in Caslon. .

Designed by John Taylor-Convery
Composed at JTC Imagineering, Santa Maria, CA

Links

Visit Leapfrog Press on Facebook
Google: Facebook Leapfrog Press
or enter:
https://www.facebook.com/pages/Leapfrog-Press/222784181103418

Leapfrog Press Website
www.leapfrogpress.com

Author Website
www.johnsmelcer.com